MURDER TO MUSIC

MARGARET NEWMAN

AGORA BOOKS

ABOUT THE AUTHOR

Margaret Newman, born in 1926 in Middlesex, was educated at Harrow County School for girls and gained a BA and MA from St. Hugh's College, Oxford.

Before writing, she worked a variety of jobs including teaching in Egypt, editing a children's magazine in London, and advising the Citizen's Advice Bureau in Twickenham. She published her first novel as Margaret Newman – a mystery novel entitled *Murder to Music*.

Newman continued publishing novels until her death in 1998, under a variety of pseudonyms and encompassing multiple genres. As Anne Melville, she focused on historical novels, including the epic wartime saga *Debutante*. Over the course of her career, she published fifty-five novels in romance, mystery, historical fiction, and children's.

ALSO BY MARGARET NEWMAN

Murder to Music

WRITING AS ANNE MELVILLE

The Lorimer Family Series
The Lorimer Line
The Lorimer Legacy
Lorimers at War
Lorimers in Love
The Last of the Lorimers
Lorimer Loyalties

The Hardie Family Series
The House of Hardie
The Daughter of Hardie
The Hardie Inheritance

Fiction
Sirocco
Alexa
Blaize
Family Fortunes
Marriage Without Love
The Dangerfield Diaries
The Tantivy Trust

A Clean Break

The Russian Tiara

Standing Alone

The Longest Silence

Role Play

The Eyes of the World

Home Run

Debutante

SHORT STORY COLLECTIONS

Snapshots

Just What I Wanted

MURDER

TO

MUSIC

This edition published in 2020 by Agora Books

First published in Great Britain by John Long in 1959

Agora Books is a division of Peters Fraser + Dunlop Ltd

55 New Oxford Street, London WC1A 1BS

CHAPTER ONE

'One of these days,' said Delia, 'you're going to answer a murder call and find when you arrive that it's from the Metro's Managing Committee.'

Detective-Superintendent Hudson laughed softly in the darkness of the car.

'I hope I arrive in time tonight, then, to carry you away from the scene of slaughter. What am I liable to find? The whole Committee stretched lifeless on the floor, surrounded by bottles of poisoned beer? Or only the lovely body of Delia Jones, transfixed by eight barbed agendas?'

'Oh no, thank you: I don't expect to be a victim myself. But there are times when I expect at every moment to become a witness.'

'Then you must increase my chances of promotion by telling me the answer in advance. Who's going to kill who?'

'Whom.'

'By that evasion I perceive that you have a guilty conscience. Obviously, you are the murderer. And the victim?'

Delia giggled.

'I've no idea. I'm only sure that Owen will be one of the two.

He has an incredible capacity for taking and giving offence—both at once usually. I say, stop! We're here!'

The car skidded violently on the wet road and came to a standstill with its front wheels on the pavement.

'Simon, really! I shan't think that your offer of a lift was so opportune after all if you are going to kill me before we arrive.'

'We *have* arrived, Delia. I'm the safest driver in London. That manoeuvre was expressly designed to bury your head in my chest, and it has been thoroughly successful. There will be a short pause while I take advantage of it.'

'I'm late,' said Delia after a rather long pause. 'And you're going to take me home again, aren't you?'

She escaped from the car and ran hastily through the rain to ring at Mrs Bainsbury's front door. Inside the house the Committee was just beginning the meeting which would, by words quickly spoken, bring death amongst its members.

Roger Bainsbury opened the door quietly and put his finger to his lips as Delia slipped past him into the hall.

'Hurry up,' he whispered. 'They've started.'

'Is everybody else here then?'

'All except the Old Man, and they're not waiting for him.'

He took her coat and threw it over the chest beneath the stairs to join the six rain-dampened mackintoshes already lying there. Delia smiled at him in the mirror as she ran her fingers through the auburn curls of her hair, flattened by the tight grip of a headscarf.

'Poor Roger. Always being pushed out of your own drawing-room for us. It's a shame.'

'Oh not really. I've got my own den—and, anyway, I push Mother out for one evening a week when the soccer club selection committee meets here, so I can't begrudge her the Metro's one night a month. Well, I expect you'll have a good fight.'

He gave her one of his quick, nervous smiles. It was three years now since he had so unpredictably withdrawn from the implications of their increasing friendship, and still he was too embarrassed in her presence ever to look her in the eyes. But Delia, who even at the time had been able to understand and accept his hesitations, could answer him now as unselfconsciously as he would have liked to speak to her.

'You never spoke a truer word.' She raised her hand in cheerful farewell and opened the door of Mrs Bainsbury's drawing-room. She paused in the doorway, for Mrs Bainsbury herself, the Committee's secretary, was rushing headlong through the Minutes of the last meeting. But Delia was not permitted to be tactful. The reading was interrupted as soon as her presence was observed, and seven pairs of eyes fixed themselves reproachfully upon her as she slid apologetically into one of Roger's home-made 'contemporary' chairs. It was uncushioned and the wooden back creaked as she tried to make herself comfortable; in the end, as on every other occasion, she abandoned the attempt and sat stiffly upright, her eyes ticking off the other occupants of the room while her ears were battered by the secretary's staccato paragraphs.

The Managing Committee of the Metropolitana, one of London's larger choral societies, may have had music in its collective soul, but it had little beauty in its face. Apart from Delia herself, whose good looks and trim figure were of what even her own father called the 'sensible' kind, only Shirley Marsden stood out at once from a first impression of dowdiness. The transitory peaches-and-cream complexion of the true blonde was displayed to its best advantage above a black sweater cut much lower than was necessary or even decent, thought Delia in disgust, for an ordinary business meeting. When Shirley (her age unfortunately fixed for ever by a mother who had wept over the first appearance of Shirley Temple) piled her hair on top of her head she attained a dignity that could make even the hardened stare. Today, however, loose curls fell in a luxuriant length. The annoying thing was that it was all natural, as untouched by the beauty salon as the slim figure which could make the most outrageous dress appear an enviable model.

And there was worse than that. If Delia could have written Shirley off as a beautiful doll, a dumb blonde, it would have been possible not to resent her. But the girl was clever; she had been brought up to have music in her bones until she knew, both by instinct and by study, whether an unlikely note in an edition was intended or misprinted, whether a horn part could be transcribed for organ without the effect being noticed, what balance of players and singers would be required for any work you might care to name, and where a few extra tenors could be found to strengthen a weak section on the night of a concert. She did not have a particularly good voice (Delia, whose soprano notes were pure and steady, was very conscious of this fact) but she recognised the lack by singing softly and, as the choir's librarian, she more than pulled her weight. Even if she had been useless, of course, she would still have been a member of the Committee, with those looks—that is, if Owen had anything to do with it; for amongst the members of the choir she was popularly and with truth known as Burr's Popsy.

Owen Burr. There was another interesting face. Sometimes the face of the dedicated musician, more often that of the ambitious young man, but always striking. The assistant conductor wore his black hair almost long enough to justify the popular impression of a musician; vividly it framed the paleness of the face in which his dark eyes darted. When, as now, he was listening inactively, his expression appeared merely to be sulky, but even those who disliked him—and they were many—were ready to admit that when he was in control of a situation he had the power to fire it with his own confidence; then every muscle was electric and those sulky eyes became compelling, able to draw music out of the two hundred men and women whom he often cursed as more recalcitrant than stones.

'Is it the Committee's wish,' said Mrs Cuthbertson, 'that I should sign these Minutes as a true record of our proceedings?'

Delia raised two fingers perfunctorily; no one else moved and the chairwoman scribbled her name without troubling to look up. As she handed the Minute Book back to the secretary, Mrs Cuthbertson breathed contentedly and settled herself more firmly in a chair several sizes too small for her. Rolls of fat leant themselves comfortably on every available support: only the stalactite hanging from her chin wobbled uncertainly as she appealed for Matters Arising. Wobbly, that was the name for Mrs Cuthbertson, thought Delia; wobbly as a body, as a chairman of committee and, above all, as a singer. It was surprising really that Owen had never managed to weed her out in the annual re-auditions which were all his own idea. Perhaps, by virtue of her office, she had quite simply excused herself from attending the ordeal, and yet it was unlike Owen to refrain from battle in the cause of musical tone—even if his adversary had been a member of the Metro since its foundation forty-two years before.

Now she was wobbling again, peering distractedly at the agenda paper on her knee. Delia, her chair creaking unbearably, strained to look over the shoulder of her neighbour, the treasurer, Robert Stanley. 'Mr Tredegar's Mass', the next item, announced itself without further explanation and Delia gasped with astonishment. The Old Man had been rumoured to be working on a choral work for the past eight years; had it actually reached a stage when one could talk about it as a fact?

'Mr Tredegar's Mass,' said Mrs Cuthbertson. 'Well, I'm sure we shall all be very pleased to hear that our conductor has now completed his important work. Of course, it is bound to make a great stir in the musical world and so I am very proud to be able to tell you that the first performance is to be entrusted to the Metropolitana, with Mr Tredegar himself of course conducting. I believe Mr Burr has some more to tell us on this subject.'

Owen looked up, glancing round at the Committee. The sulkiness left his eyes, giving him an expression of eagerness which disguised an unstable state of nerves.

'It's a good Mass,' he said. 'In C minor. The Old Man's done a really fine job this time. It's thoroughly English but right up to date, and much more lyrical than a lot of this modern stuff—reads almost like opera at times. Shirley's seen the score and she agrees with me that even the potatoes at the Metro ought to be able to manage it if they're prepared to put in a bit of hard work. We can have the Festival Hall on December 19th and the BBC jumped at the chance of a broadcast. I've let one or two of the critics know already. They'll give us a good bit of advance publicity—and I don't see why we shouldn't make it quite a social occasion too. The Old Man can rustle up a few of his posh friends and the others will start queuing for boxes before they even know what's on. It should be quite a do.'

'Well,' said Mrs Cuthbertson, 'that sounds very satisfactory, doesn't it?' She smiled happily round, her chins swaying with pleasure.

'Damned *un*satisfactory,' said Mackenzie Mortimer, a neat, precise tenor whose role on the Committee, like Delia's, was primarily to represent the views of the two hundred members of the choir; free from the responsibility of even minor office, he felt it his duty to guard the rules and constitution of the organisation at all times. 'Are you trying to tell us, Mr Burr, that you have already made a definite arrangement with the BBC on your own responsibility?'

Mrs Cuthbertson rearranged one or two of the higher rolls of flesh to turn towards the young assistant conductor.

'Mr Mortimer has a point there, of course, Mr Burr. The matter should strictly have been arranged through this Committee.'

Owen ignored her completely, his eyes flashing angrily at his critic.

'Good God, man, do you think the BBC is going to wait while you all grope your way towards the idea that there's nothing wrong with accepting a fat fee? You're not suggesting that we shouldn't *do* the work, are you? We can't possibly lose money on a concert like this.'

'Unfortunately…' The treasurer leaned back in his chair and expanded himself. 'Unfortunately, experience has shown that there is *no* type of concert on which we are unable to lose money. And if the fee is fat, the expenses no doubt will be even fatter.'

'Well, of course, I never expected *you* to be enthusiastic, Mr Stanley.' Owen's speech now was clipped, and, in the accent of his sarcasm, a touch of his Welsh childhood was betrayed. 'You are afraid, doubtless, that the bank will refuse to meet our payments and expose to the world the exact amounts which you have embezzled since the last audit.'

It's the sort of thing a schoolchild would say in fun, thought Delia, watching the treasurer seem suddenly to shrivel up as he rocked his chair back on to its four legs again. *Only his tone makes it sound so offensive. I wonder why Robert always rises—it's enough to make one wonder whether he does help himself occasionally.*

But outwardly she decided that it was time to make her contribution to the discussion, which might otherwise prolong itself indefinitely.

'Even though we may feel that Mr Burr has enough to do with the musical side of the choir and should be relieved of any administrative details by its officers,' she began smoothly, rewarded by a suspicious glower from Owen and the flicker of a smile from John Southerley, the accompanist, who sat opposite her, 'yet in this case he's only anticipated what we would have wished, hasn't he? I'm delighted that we are to have this opportunity, but we haven't long to prepare for it. May I suggest that we get down to details?'

She was rather pleased with that and accepted John Southerley's wink with a mischievous grin. The Committee settled into a familiar routine; its members had experience of everything but the requirements of this particular work, and these were supplied by Shirley.

'Tenor, bass and contralto soloists only,' she said. 'The Old Man says he can't stand these squeakers. There's one soprano solo, but it's written for a boy and he says he'll find one himself for that. Organ and piano. Strings, wood, drums and two trumpets. Possibly harp, but he might write that part in for organ.'

'Well then,' said Mrs Cuthbertson. 'Contraltos first.'

'There aren't any contraltos in England now,' said John Southerley, and the silence seemed to confirm his opinion.

'Jean Badham,' said Owen firmly.

Even Shirley looked surprised.

'I've never heard of her. Who is she?'

'The Ferrier of the future. She's not much more than a student, but already she's got a voice that will make you gasp. We can carry one unknown on an occasion like this, and we'll find her gratitude useful later when everyone wants her. She'll be cheap, too.'

No one offered any further comment; Mrs Bainsbury made a doubtful note of the name.

'Now the bass,' said Mrs Cuthbertson.

'Rolf Wenski.' The Committee seemed to be speaking in chorus. Mrs Bainsbury wrote more confidently.

'What about a tenor?'

There was another silence. Everyone knew that the tenor they would all prefer had been so exasperated by Owen's comments on the rehearsal before the last concert that he had vowed never to come near the Metro again.

'If anyone wants Davidson,' Owen said suddenly, reading their thoughts, 'I'm against it. He's going downhill fast. I heard him broadcast the other day and he was consistently half a tone sharp. I don't think he's capable of a new work like this.'

Again Delia caught the faint grin on John Southerley's face; but Shirley was speaking.

'You know, Owen, you were quite right when you said that parts of the Mass were almost operatic. Why don't we ask Cassati?'

The Committee gasped.

'But he wouldn't leave Italy just for us,' objected Mackenzie Mortimer. 'And if he did, his fee would be astronomical.'

'I happen to know that he's coming over for a gala at Covent Garden on December 24th,' Shirly replied calmly. 'He might well agree to come a few days early. The fee *would* be high, of course, but on the other hand our concert—a first performance —will be quite an occasion too; it won't do his reputation any harm to be part of it. I think he might be reasonable.'

'We could afford forty guineas, I should think,' Robert Stanley said reflectively, his fingers doodling little sums on his agenda paper.

'He won't come for *that*.' Owen spoke brusquely. 'You people seem to think that just because a man's a musician, he can't have any common sense. Cassati's the greatest tenor in the world and he's over forty. He's got his old age to think of. "Reasonable" doesn't mean "ludicrous".'

'Even with the broadcast fee coming in, fifty guineas would have to be our top offer, and that's dangerous,' said the treasurer firmly.

'God!' muttered Owen, hunching himself back once more into his armchair by the fire.

'Can we,' asked Shirley, 'instruct the secretary to engage Signor Cassati if he will come for fifty guineas or less? If not, I suppose it will have to be Davidson again.'

'That seems a very reasonable solution.' Mrs Cuthbertson looked jerkily round the room. 'Mrs Bainsbury, will you…'

'Of course.' Mrs Bainsbury was more efficient than her dowdy housewifeliness would suggest; she was writing too busily to return the chairwoman's nervous smile. 'And for the pianist?'

Everyone looked at John Southerley, a pleasant, shy young man who flushed scarlet and studied his toes.

'Well,' said Mrs Cuthbertson, beaming. 'I would like to propose that we invite our accompanist, Mr Southerley, to play the part. He gives us so much of his time and skill at our practices that I do think...'

Her voice tailed away into uncertainty once more, but she was reassured by a general murmur of agreement from the little group. Only Owen scowled, then spoke abruptly.

'It's out of the question. The part's a difficult one and we must have a professional. I suggest Bretherton.'

'But, my dear Mr Burr, Mr Southerley *is* a professional. We have all admired his recitals at the Wigmore Hall. I feel it would be ungrateful of us not to forward his career, if we can do so in a way so pleasant for ourselves.'

John rose abruptly.

'Perhaps you'd prefer me to wait outside while you discuss this.'

'There's nothing to discuss,' Owen interrupted sharply. 'It's quite out of the question. Although I may not be trusted even to buy a stamp on behalf of the choir, I presume you're not going to deny that I have the right to make decisions on artistic matters.'

'Well, you haven't really, you know, Owen,' said Mackenzie Mortimer. 'I don't want to be difficult, but that right belongs to the Old Man. The fact that you're his assistant doesn't automatically give you all his privileges. This is something that I feel is important. The choir would like to see John's name on our posters, I know, and if we can't agree on it here, then I think we ought to put it up to the Old Man himself.'

The door opened gently and Roger Bainsbury's head appeared.

'The Old Man's just arrived,' he announced quietly, and there followed an exchange of raised eyebrows and shakes of the head with his mother which Delia sadly interpreted as meaning that refreshments were being offered and rejected until later. He withdrew with a smile, and his place in the doorway was taken by Evan Tredegar, conductor-in-chief of the Metropolitana.

At the sight of the bowed white head, the heavy body, the men of the Committee rose to their feet and there ensued several minutes of bobbing up and down, of proffered arms and chairs, until the Old Man was seated. *But he's as fit as any of them*, thought Delia to herself indignantly, *seventy-nine though he may be.*

A man who could look so clumsy and dull, even apathetic, and yet could talk like a leprechaun and conduct like a child's vigorous caricature of a conductor was not a man who would win Delia's pity for senility. On the contrary, it annoyed her that he should foster the reputation of his age and should leave so much to be done by the young assistant he had appointed. She did not realise that he was in fact as lazy as he pretended to be, that his only real interest was in the composition of the large-scale works which he produced at the end of each decade. He took pleasure in conducting concert performances, but he had never been able to understand why an amateur choir should need more than the couple of rehearsals which normally sufficed for a professional orchestra, and it had been a landmark in his career when his increasing age and reputation had enabled him, eight years before, to hand the work of battering the music into the choir over to Owen Burr.

'Sorry to be late,' he muttered as he lowered himself weightily into the most comfortable chair, opposite to Owen's. 'Knew you were going to discuss the Mass; thought I'd better give you the chance to turn it down before I turned up to make it embarrassing for you.'

The Committee produced a selection of deprecatory noises.

Only Delia and John smiled across the room to each other their appreciation of the new excuse. Evan Tredegar, when he came at all to the Metro's Committee meetings, came late; it was popularly supposed that he was interested only in the beer with which the session usually ended.

'We were just discussing the question of the pianist, Mr Tredegar,' Mackenzie Mortimer said respectfully. 'Of course, the decision is entirely yours, but most of us feel that we would like John to be considered.'

Owen interrupted hurriedly before Tredegar could finish clearing his throat.

'Of course, sir, I pointed out that it would be impossible.'

'Impossible? Nothing is impossible, Owen my lad. Why should this be?'

'Obviously a more experienced player will be needed— someone like Bretherton.'

Tredegar grunted, sitting back in his chair and crossing his thick legs in front of him.

'Nonsense, my boy. Absolute nonsense. If I'd wanted Bretherton, I should have scored the part for harpsichord; fellow's no good on a modern piano. Wrote the part for John; thought it was time the Metro gave him something better to do than thump out the soprano part on two fingers. Sure he'll do it very well—eh, John?'

Delia watched the young man's face flush once more with pleasure as, with a rustle of agenda papers, the Committee moved on to the next business. But there was resentment in his eyes as well, *and it's not surprising*, she thought, *when Owen's done his best to humiliate him.* She moved her eyes to Owen himself, and at the glance she shivered. Resentment was too mild a word for the expression in those dark Welsh eyes. They were fixed intently on Evan Tredegar, and every flicker was impregnated with hate.

CHAPTER TWO

Simon watched from the car as Delia stood for a moment on Mrs Bainsbury's doorstep and smiled at a young man—a very young man, he noticed bitterly. They chatted briefly together; then Delia shook her head in reply to some question of her companion's and, glancing towards the road, recognised Simon's car and waved.

'Still alive, then?' said Simon as he opened the car door for her, repressing with some difficulty the question he would really have liked to ask.

'Just about. Tired, though.' Delia flopped heavily into the seat and slammed the door. 'Why didn't you come in and fetch me?'

'I didn't want to spoil the fun. There's nothing like the arrival of a policeman for drying up all the really spiteful conversation and producing on every face that "all friends together and I was only doing twenty-nine-and-a-half, officer" sort of smirk.'

He began to drive at a leisurely pace towards Delia's suburban home. Delia was genuinely tired and sat silently; Simon glanced sideways at her and smiled.

'Come along, tell me all. You know how I love your gossip. Who is Owen's great enemy today?'

'Oh, it varies from moment to moment. I think he managed to be rude to everyone except Shirley and me tonight.'

'Well, at least that shows *some* sense of discrimination. You don't mean to say that even your Old Man came under fire, though?'

Delia considered for a moment.

'No, I don't think Owen actually *said* anything to him, although there was one moment when looks were trying very hard to kill. On the whole, Mrs Bainsbury came off worst—it seemed rather hard when we were all guests in her house.'

'Mrs Bainsbury? I always get these women mixed up. Is she the chairman or the secretary?'

'Secretary. She's quite pleasant though I find her a little dull —one of these fiftyish women who devote their lives to their sons. Mind you, I think she's quite sensible about it. Roger's really rather a man's man; he likes playing team games and drinking at the local and making furniture and television sets and gadgets, but whenever he gets interested in a girl, she makes him bring her home to hear a little speech about wanting to see her dear boy settled down. She'll always have the choir business to fall back on, of course; it must be very nearly a full-time job.'

'How do you know all this?' asked Simon carefully.

'Oh I was one of Roger's girls for about three months. That was how I got on to the Committee. The members' representatives are supposed to be chosen by the singers in the choir just to put their point of view without holding any office, but in fact, of course, nobody ever knows anyone else's name or anything about them, so usually the secretary puts a couple of people up and the choir votes for them like a string of obedient sausages. Roger saw me at a concert one day and saw to it that I was one of the names for the next year. That's all.'

'I see,' said Simon coldly. Delia glanced across at him, startled.

'Oh, Simon, don't be *silly*. That was three years ago, and anyway he gave me up after a couple of months. I believe he always does. He had a bad war, and he was too young when it started to have made much of a life for himself; now he seems too frightened of responsibility to try. I felt rather sorry for him really. He was wanting so hard to fall in love and he simply couldn't manage it. Sometimes I used to be naughty and just stand while he tried to persuade himself to kiss me goodnight. But he never did.'

'Never?'

'Never ever.' She put her hand on his knee and squeezed it gently. 'I think you'd be surprised if you knew how very few people have ever been allowed to kiss me goodnight, Simon.'

He gave her a quick smile. 'Sorry, Delia. Sometimes it really hurts to think that I've missed twenty-nine years of your life. I would so much have liked to know you while I was still young.'

'You *are* young,' said Delia emphatically. 'If anyone tells *me* that I'm not young when I'm only thirty-eight, there'll be plenty of trouble.'

Swaying gently from one side of the road to the other, Simon found a hand to enclose hers, and they smiled into each other's eyes.

'Well,' he said at last. 'Tell me more about your Mrs Bainsbury. Is she a good secretary?'

'Absolutely terrific. She never seems to put a foot wrong. It's quite a job, you know, keeping two hundred singers happy and getting the right number of highly unbusinesslike musicians to turn up at the right concert-hall on the right day with more than a vague idea of the work they are due to perform. Not to mention dealing with printers, agencies, advertising, copyright holders and all the rest of it. All the Committee does is to mention a few names and then say: "And everything else as usual, Mrs Bainsbury; it seemed most satisfactory last time."

And the next time it seems equally satisfactory, but I'm sure an immense amount of work must go into it. She does it all for love —and yet Owen treats her like a junior shorthand-typist. It makes my blood boil sometimes.'

'Why doesn't she resign, just to show him?'

'Strictly confidentially, I think she's got a bit of a thing about the Old Man. In fact, I did once hear a bit of gossip about them in their younger days, but it was too vague to be worth repeating. Anyhow, she certainly hero-worships him now—can hardly keep her eyes off him. We even get such gems in the Minutes as: "Following an inspired suggestion by the conductor-in-chief, the Committee agreed that...".' They laughed together.

'And is the adoration reciprocated?' asked Simon.

'Oh, far from it. He's rather testy with her, in fact—gives the impression that he hasn't any use for her. That's what makes Owen feel that he can be as rude as he likes. But the Old Man knows her value as a secretary, he never goes too far.'

'Unlike Owen? You haven't told me about their row yet.'

'Yes, it was a real blaze-up. To look at her, you'd never think she had a temper, but it came out tonight all right. For two hours she just sat there, making notes, looking efficient, nodding her head, and then suddenly she was spitting like a cat. It was about the Old Man's Mass; we'd discussed it at the beginning of the meeting and then we came back to it at the end, because she wanted to check one or two details for the publicity.'

'By the Old Man's Mass do you mean the quantity of flesh which is his habitual companion? It seems to me rather a delicate subject for a Committee.'

'Silly! He's written a Mass. A choral work. In C minor.'

'I see—but you could hardly expect me to know that by instinct. Is he a Catholic, then?'

Delia looked surprised. 'I don't think so. I imagine he just wanted to challenge the great composers on their own ground.

It's designed for the concert-hall rather than the church, I gather —massed voices and quite a big orchestra. You know, under all his laziness, I think the Old Man cares quite a lot about his reputation. Not as a conductor so much, but as a composer.'

'Well, his reputation is fairly high, isn't it? I should have thought he came into the category of household names.'

'I suspect that he wants the household name to have a handle. I may be quite wrong, of course, but there's been a rumour going round for some weeks that he's under consideration for a knighthood in the New Year Honours. Mind you, he deserves it all right, but I wouldn't be *too* greatly surprised to learn that he'd started the rumour himself in the hope that its foundation might come later. And he's chosen a good time. He'll be eighty next March, and if there's one thing the British public likes to give honours for, it's survival into old age. I wouldn't be at all surprised if he hasn't held up the Mass just so that he can make a splash at exactly the right time. The whole thing would appeal to his sense of humour.'

'Has he got one of those? The last time I saw him, he looked half dead.'

'He's very much alive, as a matter of fact. I like him. I only wish he wouldn't leave so much to that beast Owen. I'm not saying that there's anything wrong with Owen as a conductor, not technically, but he does put people's backs up so, and it's awfully difficult to sing well when you're annoyed. Of course, it must be very frustrating for him, too. He has to do all the work at practices and then the Old Man steps in and collects all the Press raves on the night. Still, I refuse to be sorry for him. He is a beast.'

'And has friend Owen ever taken you home so that his mother can tell you how much she wants him to settle down?'

The smile faded from Delia's face as she looked across at her companion.

'Darling, is that still rankling? Please forget it.' There was a moment's silence before she went on to answer his question. 'No. He hasn't got a mother, and he *has* got Shirley. I'm no more to him than a soprano occasionally suspected of sharpness— musically, I mean.'

'And what is Shirley to him?'

'Now you're leaving the field of gossip and starting on scandal. I have no idea, and I don't particularly want to find out. If you don't slow down, you'll be halfway to Scotland in a minute.'

'Good heavens, is this your place already?' Simon stopped with a jerk which rocked them both forwards. He turned off the engine and put his arm round her shoulders.

'Am I being invited in?'

'No, I don't think you are. It's after midnight already and we both have to get up tomorrow.'

'Well, stay here a little, then.'

She glanced at the glowing upper window of the house.

'I'd better not, Simon. I see Dad's awake, and he'll know it's us.'

'I don't see how that matters.'

'Don't you just? He read one of the Kinsey reports last year, and ever since he has regarded any parked automobile with the greatest suspicion. Say goodnight nicely.'

He kissed her tightly. Simon had become a widower at the age of twenty-two, only four months after his marriage. Since then he had lost the habit of taking happiness lightly. He hated each parting from Delia, feeling that one day he might find he would never see her again. Something of this she understood, and she was gentle with him, but at last she put his hands aside and slipped out of the car. As she stood for a second with the door open, touching her lips with her fingers, he made a last appeal for her company.

'But you can't go yet, Delia. You never told me in the end what Owen and Mrs Bainsbury were quarrelling about.'

'So now you'll never know—unless you use your detective training to deduce it all from nothing. It won't really keep you awake at nights though, will it?'

'Not that, perhaps,' he said miserably, and then the door of the car slammed, echoing down the wet and empty street.

CHAPTER THREE

'But I think it's wonderful, quite wonderful, my dear. How could you have kept it to yourself for six weeks? Another work by Evan Tredegar, and the Metro to sing it. Aren't you all just too thrilled?'

Mrs Bainsbury smiled her agreement and poured another cup of tea for her friend.

'Yes, we're very pleased. I do wish you were still in the choir to sing it with us, Janet. It was quite unnecessary of Owen to push you out when you'd been a member for such a long time. There aren't many founder-members left now—in fact, I think that Mrs Cuthbertson must be almost the only one. That boy has no sense of respect.'

Mrs Sheraton-Smith sighed a little. 'Yes, it would have been nice. But you know, dear Maude, you mustn't get too angry with young Owen on my behalf. He's quite right from his point of view. He wants to give pleasure to the people who come to hear the concerts, not to the members of the choir, and it's quite a reasonable way of looking at it. And there's no doubt about it, I'm afraid; I've found it increasingly difficult to hear properly since that horrible bomb. I'm not very much use as a singer anymore.'

'But you hear everything I say perfectly well, Janet. Have some of this cake. It's a new recipe and most successful. And there are very few works that you would have to learn from the beginning like Evan's Mass; you know the old favourites off by heart already.'

'Thank you, dear. Yes, I do hear what you say, but not how you say it. It all seems to be on one note. So I should never have any idea of whether I was singing sharp or flat—in fact, I might be several tones away from the right note, and from what Owen said to me at that audition, I must assume that I was.'

'He had no right to talk to you like that.' Mrs Bainsbury attacked a slice of chocolate cake with her knife, chopping it sharply into fingers and then squares.

'Isn't that what we pay him for? I admit I was upset at the time, but that was a long time ago. Now I just try to help in other ways, since I can't sing. Tell me, dear—I was so interested when you told me on the telephone that you were going to ask Cassati. Will he come?'

'Unfortunately not. I had a letter from his agent this morning, sneezing politely at our offer of forty guineas. I hoped that he might be willing to haggle a little and settle for fifty at last. But not a bit of it. He just sent a printed brochure with a note attached to say that Signor Cassati's fee for single performances was never less than a hundred guineas. So it looks as though we shall have to appeal to Davidson. I'm sure he'll come, actually, if we can arrange it so that his face can be saved. I heard yesterday that he'd been trying to get Evan to lunch with him.'

'Is this Cassati?' Mrs Sheraton-Smith picked up a glossy leaflet and studied with interest the photograph on its cover. The face it showed was fat and thick-lipped, with scant hair greased flatly down. The eyes were small and lifeless; the only glint came from a tooth, presumably of gold, which showed itself beneath the posed smile. 'It *is* a pity they run to fat so, isn't it? But somebody was telling me the other day that they *need* the fat to increase the resonance, or something like that; it sounded quite reasonable at the time. But listen to me, Maude. I think you ought to have Cassati. After all, this *is* a special occasion; one wants to be a little *different* at such times, don't you agree, dear? I mean, Davidson's first-class, of course, but one can hear him somewhere almost any day of the week. And everyone tells me that Cassati is really someone quite exceptional. My maid—the one who goes to evening classes, you know—she has one of his Pagliacci records and she sits in the kitchen on her free afternoon and plays it with the tears simply streaming down her face. Of course, she hasn't seen *this!*' Mrs Sheraton-Smith poked a disdainful finger at the brochure. 'But she certainly made me wish that I could appreciate a little more what she was hearing. So you must have him for your concert.'

Mrs Bainsbury sighed. 'But Janet, we simply can't afford it. Even with special prices there's a top limit to what we can expect to get, and, if possible, we want to give Evan a much larger fee than usual—to celebrate, in a manner of speaking. It's no good saying that we must have Cassati when we can't pay his fee.'

'You interrupted me, Maude dear. I wasn't going to ask you to afford him. I've been thinking this over ever since you first mentioned it to me; of course I knew that you would never get him for forty guineas, but I thought it wouldn't do any harm to try. Now, if the Metro can go up to fifty, I'll pay the other fifty myself.'

Mrs Sheraton-Smith sat back in her chair, enjoying the sight of her friend struggling for words; then with a heavily ringed hand she helped herself to another chocolate biscuit.

'Janet, you really are too generous. You've put too much money into the Metro already. Only last year you gave us thirty pounds to pay our debts after that foggy night when no one would come.'

'My dear, I happen to *have* a lot of money, and now that
Geoffrey's dead the best thing I can do is to give it to people
who will use it for something worthwhile.'

She had pronounced the name 'Geoffrey' carefully, as if she
were practising it, and Mrs Bainsbury looked at her friend
compassionately. It had taken Mrs Sheraton-Smith almost three
years to recover from the breakdown which followed the news
that her only son had died in Italy, the son who had been her
whole life since his father's death when the boy was still a baby;
it was still not a subject on which she very often cared to talk,
even to the mother of Roger, who had been Geoffrey's closest
friend. Mrs Bainsbury hesitated a moment and then made her
voice as brisk and business-like as possible.

'Then that's wonderful, Janet dear. I'll tell Robert Stanley and
write off to the agent straight away. Everyone will be so
grateful.'

'Oh no. That is not what I want at all. I shan't let you have
the money unless the whole thing is kept completely secret. You
can arrange it, can't you? The agent will have to send half the
bill to Mr Stanley and the other half to me. The Committee can
simply think that you have been lucky to get the man for fifty
guineas.'

Mrs Bainsbury looked doubtful. 'It might lead to a lot of
complications. If people think that Cassati is available at that fee
he'll be deluged with offers, which will infuriate him. The Metro
itself might want him again, and then it would be essential to
tell them.'

'In that extreme case you would have to talk about a "friend
of the choir", without giving my name. I don't see that there
should be any difficulty and I am sure that you can deal with it.
In any case, that is the condition on which I offer the money. I
am sorry if it will force you to cook your files, but I must
insist.'

'Well, of course you're quite entitled to do so, and I'll do my best. But why must it be so secret?'

Mrs Sheraton-Smith rose straight-backed from her chair. 'I don't want to embarrass anyone, Maude. Your young Owen is not quite such a boor as you occasionally appear to think him. He has his own feelings and he sometimes appreciates those of other people, though he doesn't seem able to stop himself hurting them. He knows that he hurt me a little when he made me leave the choir and I don't want him to think that I'm collecting coals of fire for his head. I know it means a lot to his pride that you should invite Cassati and not Davidson, and I have a little sympathy for him. He's going to be a very great musician one of these days, Maude, so we must forgive him if he isn't always very great as a man.'

Mrs Bainsbury stared in incredulity. 'Of all the reasons which you might have had for giving away fifty guineas, that really seems to me the most difficult to believe.'

Her friend paused for a moment in her progress to the door. 'But then, Maude, forgiveness is something which you have never been able to practise, isn't it—perhaps you have never even wanted to do so.'

She left the house with the dignity of an old lady, bowing her head slightly in thanks for her entertainment. Mrs Bainsbury was left standing in the hall, still uncomprehending. When she returned to the drawing-room she found Roger there; he had returned from work to enter the house by the back door, and now he too was standing very still, looking, as he always did, a little over-dressed in his neat office suit—the cricket flannels or soccer shorts which he so much preferred were the only clothes which ever seemed appropriate on his compact, muscular body. He turned now as his mother entered.

'Are you starting to collect a Rogues' Gallery?' he asked quietly, pointing at the brochure which lay on the tea-tray. 'He looks like someone wanted for White Slave Trafficking.'

'My dear Roger, he's a singer. A very eminent singer. He's going to sing in Evan's Mass with us.'

'Can you afford to bring such eminent singers all the way from Italy?'

'Well, not really, but...' Mrs Bainsbury hesitated, looked at her son, and then said confidentially: 'I should think it's all right to tell you since you don't belong to the choir, but keep it to yourself. Janet's paying half his fee for us.'

Roger looked startled, almost unbelieving. 'Aunt Janet!' Then he laughed shortly. 'I shouldn't have thought she'd be too keen on encouraging Italians.'

'Because of Geoffrey, you mean? Well, I don't think she would hate all Italians just because one Italian bullet killed him. You don't, do you, just because they took you prisoner?'

'Not all of them, no, but I wasn't killed. Anyway, if you want him, I'm glad you're going to have him. What's his name? Cassati. Sounds like an ice-cream. By the way, talking of the Metro, I saw your Owen in the lunch hour. It looked to me as if young Shirley is about to get left at the altar. He was being *very* friendly with a neat little brunette. I wouldn't fancy giving the push to a girl like Shirley myself. I've seen her being angry with someone whose only crime was to lose a hired copy of a score, so what she's like in a real crisis I shudder to think.'

'Not "my" Owen, please, Roger. Is it your selection committee tonight?'

'Yes please. That's why I came in, to get the room ready. Have we any beer in the house?'

'No. You'll have to get some. I'm afraid I haven't time now. I must write some letters before the practice.'

TWO HOURS LATER MRS BAINSBURY, neatly unremarkable in black, caught a bus to the bleak rehearsal rooms in which the choir met every Tuesday. She was, as always, the first arrival, and she sat by the door as the rest of the singers appeared. She knew the name of each and ticked it off neatly in the long brown register. Those who came after the starting time would lose their mark for the evening, but there were few of these, for few would willingly face the sarcastic comments or the even more devastating silence with which Owen would watch them to their seats. Punctuality had also a cash value, for a singer who obtained the full qualification of marks in the rehearsals for any particular concert would be awarded a free ticket for that concert, which might be given to a friend. This system of Sunday School bribery had been originated by Evan Tredegar in the days when he was the active conductor of all the choir's practices; although the treasurer might complain and the singers themselves (few of whom ever qualified) gently mock, no one had ever dared to suggest that the practice should be dropped.

As usual, Owen came early and fidgeted in his seat on the platform for ten minutes, glancing at his watch and rustling through the pages of the score. At the stroke of half-past seven Mrs Bainsbury closed her brown book and nodded at him. Within a second the sopranos were being coaxed upwards into a scale. The practice had begun.

The Mass in C Minor would present few difficulties to the critics, but it was not an easy one to sing. Throughout the chorus work there ran a strong melodic line, but it switched abruptly from part to part. No note could be expected, no mark of expression could be taken for granted. Mrs Bainsbury, in her front-row seat, concentrated hard, wishing that she could lose herself sometimes in the harmony, as was possible in a Bach Mass; instead, even after six weeks of practice, she had to pay almost as much attention to the score as if she were still sight-reading.

Next door to her Delia Jones sang a wrong note and clucked

impatiently to herself, ringing the bar with her pencil. Owen tapped impatiently with his baton.

'We have been practising the Credo now for six weeks,' he said, 'and there is still a soprano who does not know the difference between F and F sharp.' His eyes swept the front row of the sopranos. 'Miss Jones, would you please sing by yourself from letter B.'

Mrs Bainsbury, beside her, felt rather than saw the sudden flush on Delia's face and sympathised with her; she would not herself have cared to sing a solo in front of the full choir, especially when it was inflicted as a punishment. For a few seconds there was silence and then Owen spoke icily again.

'Please do not keep us waiting, Miss Jones. I hope you do not imagine that your membership of the Managing Committee exempts you from paying attention to what you are singing. We are all waiting for you.'

Mrs Bainsbury glanced across at Delia; her flush was of temper now and her knuckles showed the whiteness of the bone as she gripped her score. But she sang the bars for which Owen had asked, clearly and note-perfect; only when she had finished did her lips tighten with anger.

'Thank you very much, Miss Jones. I'm sure you are very sorry to have wasted the choir's time and will be more careful in future. Now everybody from A please, and no piano. Just a chord to start them.'

The choir began the chorus once more, but unhappily. The tenors, depleted by an outbreak of sore throats, struggled to the middle and collapsed, smiling gratefully at the accompanist when he came to their rescue by joining in with their part. But Owen was not so pleased; once again the tap of his baton brought the choir to an uneasy silence.

'Mr Southerley, I particularly asked that there should be no accompaniment this time. Would you care to remember that you are not here as a concert pianist but to assist me under my direction. It's impossible for the choir to cope with all these difficulties. Ten minutes' break.'

There was a buzz of conversation. Only Owen himself sat silently alone on his platform, frowning at the music before him as he scribbled notes in its margins.

'He's in a pretty vicious mood today, isn't he?' said Delia. 'I hate having to sing by myself, and it was only a slip. It isn't as if I make mistakes all the time.'

Mrs Bainsbury smiled sympathetically, but before she could answer she was interrupted by John Southerley, who had walked over from the piano and squatted down on the floor close to her chair.

'Will you tell me something, Mrs Bainsbury?' he asked. 'Is my name actually in print yet in any of the publicity for this damned Mass?'

The secretary looked at him in surprise: she had never heard him swear before.

'Not yet, as a matter of fact. We still haven't fixed the tenor, so I've held up the posters. But the Festival Hall leaflet for December will be going to press this week. You're not regretting that you were engaged for it, I hope.'

'I certainly am. As long as you haven't actually announced it, I shall write to the Old Man and say that I'd prefer not to play.'

'Oh, John, don't do that.' Delia had turned towards them, her own humiliation forgotten in this new dismay. 'Sorry to interrupt, but I couldn't help overhearing. He'll be so disappointed because he wrote it for you. Why do you want to back out now?'

'Why do you think? Because I won't go on working with Owen Burr, that's why. I've had enough of these rehearsals, and I can't very well expect to keep the concert job if I walk out of this one; even the Old Man would jib at that. But by God I'll make my reputation for myself—I don't intend to be indebted to *him* for anything.'

He jerked his head resentfully towards the platform. Delia leaned forward eagerly.

'Don't you see, that's exactly what he wants. He's jealous because you're as good a musician as he is, and younger; he wants to stop you playing in the concert by provoking you to back out yourself. You must hang on, John, to spite him. Then you can resign afterwards if you want to.'

The accompanist looked hesitatingly at Mrs Bainsbury, who smiled at him.

'It will put you in the wrong if you walk out in the middle of a season, you know; and I think you will regret having thrown up a great opportunity in anger. We all want you to have this chance.'

John smiled his boyish smile as he stood up.

'I suppose you're right. But one of these days...'

He stopped suddenly as he noticed Owen approaching. But the assistant conductor ignored him completely and spoke only to Delia.

'It was a pity it had to be you,' he said. 'But now that people know the notes, more or less, they're beginning to get casual. I decided that I should have to make an example of the next careless singer I noticed, just to show the others what might happen to them. I fancy we shall notice the improvement now.'

He strolled back to his platform and Mrs Bainsbury turned to her neighbour.

'I think, Delia dear, that that was Owen's idea of an apology.'

'One of these days,' said Delia through tight lips, 'he's going to be rude just once too often—and then perhaps he'll find that there isn't time for an apology.'

CHAPTER FOUR

'Hello,' said Delia, and paused. 'Hello. Hello. Oh, Simon you clot, press Button A.'

There was a rattle of coins and Simon's voice spoke apologetically.

'It's funny that I should *always* forget, isn't it? I mean, once or twice would be normal, but *always.* I must ask a psychiatrist what it means.'

'Simon darling, at any other time I would stand for hours and listen to your burbling, but I must dash. Today's the great day—we're doing the Mass tonight and I'm due at the Festival Hall to rehearse at nine.'

'What a ghastly hour to make music. Is this another of Owen's little foibles?'

'Far from it; he's livid. Apparently, it's the penalty for choosing the Saturday before Christmas. There's a children's carol concert in the afternoon, and they can't decorate for it until we finish our rehearsal. Anyway, did you phone up for any special reason?'

'Yes; it's about your concert as a matter of fact. We've been sent a Christmas present of four new men, so I've decided that I deserve a week-end off duty.'

'You certainly do. It's been weeks. Does that mean that you can come to the Mass after all?'

'Don't see how I can escape it now, do you? Can you get me a ticket?'

'I should think so. I'll certainly try. Any preferences?'

'Which side of the hall will you be on?'

'Right as we face,' said Delia. 'Left as the audience sees us.'

'Then I want a seat in the front row on the left.'

'I can tell you now that the front row is sold out. That was part of Mrs Bainsbury's allocation and she told me on Tuesday that they were all gone. But I'll see what I can do. Goodbye then.'

'Hoy! I haven't finished yet. What about dinner with me beforehand at the Festival Hall?'

Delia considered. 'I'm not sure that I shall want to eat very much before singing. And I shall be in evening dress, of course.'

There was a groan at the other end of the line.

'Never mind. For you I will even dress. Seven o'clock in the restaurant, then. Goodbye.'

Delia flew for her bus, which deposited her at Waterloo at five to nine. She hurried anxiously to the hall, and the lift at the artists' entrance flashed her upwards.

'There's a cloakroom down there,' the man pointed and closed the doors before Delia could ask for any further information. She glanced at her watch and decided not to risk being late but to go straight to her seat. She turned hesitantly to the left and started to wander down a door-less passage. It led only to a flight of stairs, so she turned back and walked more quickly in the opposite direction. There was still no sign of the inside of the auditorium and several minutes had passed before she found someone who could direct her.

'Down the stairs, left and right,' he said concisely, leaving

Delia to curse the lift which had brought her too high. 'They haven't started.'

As she approached, however, she thought she heard the sound of music and automatically she quickened her step. A trolley was trundled along the passage and she flattened herself in a doorway. The door opened slightly behind her and she heard Owen's voice, speaking into a telephone.

'Certainly I haven't changed my mind,' he was saying. 'And it's being broadcast, after all. Damn it all, don't forget what you're going to get out of it.' There was a pause, and Owen spoke more testily. 'Well, they'll just have to accept it, won't they?'

Delia passed on her way, idly curious but more anxious not to arrive after the Old Man had started to rehearse. She came into the hall at last. The orchestra was seated in full strength, playing bored little runs to itself. Higher up, the members of the choir circulated, most of them crowded round the secretary who, with both arms outstretched, held an enormous sheet of paper. There was no sign of Evan Tredegar.

Delia joined the crowd and found that her place was to be in the front row, between Shirley and Mrs Bainsbury.

'I see the Committee will be well in evidence,' she remarked jokingly to the secretary, for Mrs Cuthbertson, Robert Stanley and Mackenzie Mortimer had also been allocated front seats. 'I'm not sure that it's wise to put Mrs Cuthbertson there though, is it? She's usually tucked away at the back.'

Mrs Bainsbury looked momentarily startled.

'Well,' she said defensively. 'The Committee has to do a lot of hard work. I don't see why it shouldn't be rewarded at a time like this by having a good view. You haven't seen Evan, have you? It isn't like him to be late for a concert rehearsal.'

Delia shook her head and found her seat. The hall was cold and empty; a little group of men sitting alone at the back of the Terrace Stalls only emphasised its emptiness. Suddenly there was a flutter of applause from the contraltos; a large figure appeared from the artists' door and walked heavily over to a seat in front of the sopranos. Delia craned her neck. So this was the great Cassati. She twitched her nose in instinctive dislike; the man was gross, his piggish eyes almost hidden in the pale fleshiness of his face. He wore woollen knitted gloves and a muffler with his black suit, and despite them he seemed cold and bad-temperedly impatient. Like Mrs Bainsbury, Delia wondered why the Old Man was late. The orchestra would certainly depart in a body on the first stroke of twelve, so every second lost was money wasted.

At that moment Owen appeared, almost at a run. To Delia's surprise he stepped on to the rostrum and tapped sharply with his baton. The organ boomed an A; there was a moment's scraping of violins and then silence.

'I thought the Old Man always took the orchestra rehearsal himself,' Delia whispered to Mrs Bainsbury, but before there was time for a reply Owen was making the explanation himself.

'I am very sorry to have to tell you that Mr Tredegar is ill. I have just had a telephone message from him regretting that he will not be able to conduct today's concert. He has asked me to do so in his place, since I am already completely familiar with the score and with the choir, and he has sent his best wishes for a good performance. I have no doubt that he will be listening to us on his wireless in bed tonight and I'm sure we shall all do our best to make him feel that he is hearing a great work worthily performed.'

He smiled at the choir and Delia thought with surprise that she did not ever remember having noticed him smile before. Even this attempt was made more with the teeth than with the eyes, although there was a glint in the latter which disquieted her. She turned to speak to Mrs Bainsbury, but the older woman was staring ahead of her with a look almost of hopelessness on her face.

The rustle of sympathetic whispering which Owen's announcement had caused died away and the baton tapped sharply once more.

'We'll leave the orchestral introduction for the moment. Chorus stand, please. Number Two.'

A single violin, pure and plaintive, broke the silence and, very softly, the voices of the singers stole into the Kyrie. They rose to a crescendo and then died away suddenly as they had been taught to do. Above them one single voice rose and flowed, so clear and liquid that Delia almost ceased to sing in her admiration of its beauty. Was it possible that such a gross creature could make so perfect a sound? Delia had never before heard a voice like this; Caruso, Gigli, Cassati himself she had heard on gramophone records, but those sounds could not compare with these, which seemed to ride so lightly on the clear sunbeams of the air. The choir's part ended, but the voice of the tenor rose effortlessly; it seemed to hold in its smooth notes a man's broken heart. The melody fell, whispering sadly away, and from the other side of the platform the voice of a boy, clear, yet trembling a little with nervousness, answered the plea of the man. As these notes too died away, leaving once more only a single violin, Delia felt tears pricking her eyes. She pulled her chin inwards until the silence which followed the last note was broken by a cacophony of re-tuning. Then she turned to Shirley, her eyes shining.

'I didn't know it was going to be like that,' she said. 'He makes it all sound as if he meant it, too.'

They turned their heads together to watch the tenor as he settled himself on his chair, a thick roll of fat appearing round his collar as he huddled his short neck into the warmth of his scarf and coat. But they had no time to study him, for Owen was already preparing to start the next chorus.

. . .

IT WAS eleven o'clock before they were allowed a break. Delia slipped out thankfully, making for the box office. As she did so, she recognised one of the group of listeners as Roger Bainsbury and stopped for a word with him.

'Hello, Roger. Can't you wait till tonight?'

'Unfortunately, I can't come tonight. We're playing an away match at Oxford this afternoon. It would be quite a scramble to get back anyway, and this particular match usually turns into a bit of a party. If I were really musical, no doubt I'd manage it somehow, but, as it is, I thought I could probably get enough from a rehearsal to answer Mother's questions.'

'And what do you make of it?' she asked. 'You look as if you're finding it quite an experience.' He was trying to smile at her, but his face was pale and Delia, a little emotional herself from the impact of music which seemed quite different from what she had practised in the bleak rehearsal-room, sympathised with him.

'Experience is the word,' he said quietly. 'I hadn't expected anything like this. There doesn't seem to be much relationship between music and the ordinary world, does there?'

'That's a question which requires several days to answer,' Delia laughed, 'and I've only got about two minutes to get to the box office and back. Hope you win your match. Goodbye for now.'

She hurried down, using the stairways provided for the audience this time instead of facing again the back-stage labyrinth. All seats had been sold for the evening, she was told except for a few beside the organ and behind the choir; but there was luckily one returned ticket, a seat in one of the lower front boxes on the left-hand side of the auditorium. Simon would be sitting almost above her there; he could hardly ask for anything better. She pocketed the ticket and returned to her seat.

.   .   .

THE LAST HOUR of the practice did not go so smoothly. The contralto soloist, a petite, dark-haired young woman clearly suffering from nerves, came in a bar too soon in her last solo; Owen promptly swore at the leader of the orchestra and only a hasty apology prevented the tired players from walking out in a body. Then came the last chorus, which was introduced by five bars which the contraltos were to sing unaccompanied by the orchestra. They began quietly enough but, as Owen pulled at them to increase the volume, a vibrato of a peculiarly grating character appeared. Shirley giggled slightly as Owen tapped his baton, made a sarcastic comment and began once more at the beginning.

'Bet I know who it is,' she whispered to Delia. 'Mrs Bainsbury really ought to have put her in the back row; it mightn't sound so bad there.'

Again the volume increased, and with it the vibrato. Owen hammered the score with his hand until the contraltos became guiltily silent.

'I cannot put up with this atrocious noise any longer,' he said furiously, tossing back the black lock of hair which had fallen forward over his eyes. 'If it is uncontrollable, then it must go. Mrs Cuthbertson, I must ask you to leave the choir now and not sing with it tonight. Miss Green, will you come forward and take her place in the front row, please.'

There was a gasp of dismay from the choir. With great dignity Mrs Cuthbertson picked up her handbag and walked across in front of the choir and out of the hall. She did not speak, but Delia noticed that her hands were trembling, while tears of humiliation quivered on her cheeks.

'Poor old girl,' said Shirley. 'She'll never be able to come back into the choir now. It will be a blow to her, even if it does make our committee meetings run more smoothly. Still, it really was rather an awful noise.'

'He needn't have done it so publicly, though,' protested Delia.

'It must have been a frightful slap in the face. He could have told her quietly afterwards. I think it's very hard. I'd be furious in her place.'

There was no time to say anything more; for the third time the contraltos made their lone entry, to be joined first by the other voices and then by the full orchestra. But the choir had been upset by the incident; it sang lifelessly and a little flat. Owen glanced at his watch and dismissed them; it was ten to twelve.

'We'll just run through the introduction and epilogue,' he told the orchestra.

Delia picked up her things and looked at Shirley.

'Coming?' she asked.

The blonde shook her head.

'I'll stay here to the end. I expect I'll be having lunch with Owen. See you tonight.'

Delia hurried lightly down the steps. As the door closed behind her the sounds of an eager, lyrical marching movement were abruptly cut off; she tried to imagine, as she ran, what would come after it.

CHAPTER FIVE

Delia looked at herself in the mirror and patted her hair approvingly; the pale blue blouse and midnight blue skirt and sash which formed the concert uniform of the Metro singers were becoming to her. She smiled happily. The restaurant had been packed with diners expensively dressed as for a great occasion and, in the hall, the Press photographers were still flashing at new arrivals. There was a general atmosphere of excitement which made it impossible that the evening should be a failure.

For Delia herself, it was already a success. Simon, intoxicated by the prospect of being actually able to enjoy the free time to which he was in theory entitled, had turned their dinner together into a feast of happiness. He had seemed almost a boy again as he smiled across the table and Delia was convinced that very soon now—perhaps as he drove her home after the concert —he would ask her to marry him. She had been too wise to hurry him, even though she had known both his wishes and her own for some time, but she was glad, deeply glad, that he had at last arrived at the point of decision.

She hummed a few bars of the Mass as she looked at

herself, her eyes shining. All around her the other women of the choir were jostling; some nervous, some expectant, most concerned chiefly with the colour of their lips. Over her shoulder she caught sight of Shirley, and her eyebrows rose in appreciation. Although the blonde librarian wore the same dress as every other singer, on her it was cut to seem more seductive than demure, tight enough to show a warm round-ness that even Delia could appreciate. Above the neat blue blouse she wore a tight circle of glittering diamanté and her hair seemed to glitter too, as if it had been sprinkled with silver dust.

Probably it has, thought Delia to herself and turned round to confront this vision in the flesh.

'Shirley, you look wonderful,' she began, but Shirley walked straight past her, her mouth hard and her eyes flashing like her necklace, but with anger.

Delia stared after her in surprise, then raised an eyebrow in enquiry at Mrs Bainsbury, who was standing nearby.

'What's bitten Shirley? Has she missed her dinner?'

'Well, as a matter of fact, I think perhaps she has. I can guess what's wrong, I think—but I ought not to mention it. After all, I was not really supposed to hear.'

'Oh come, Mrs Bainsbury, you can't throw out a dark hint like that and then stop, it's too tantalising. I want to know all the scandal.'

'Well, I do think she's had rather a—a severe quarrel with Owen this morning. I happened to be passing his room soon after the rehearsal ended and they were speaking so loudly—shouting, really—that I couldn't help—oh, good gracious, it's nearly five to eight. Excuse me; I must get everyone into line.' She bustled off, shouting above the general noise, 'Front row sopranos please, quickly.'

Delia smiled to herself as she moved through the crowd to take her place in the line. She was so pleased with the state of her own affairs that she could not spare very much thought for Shirley's.

A little self-consciously they filed into the hall. There was not an empty seat to be seen, nor even any unused standing room. Delia's eyes went first to the box where Simon sat. He saw that she was looking and raised his hand to his lips. Her heart bounded; this was going to be a wonderful evening. All around her the singers were exchanging the names of those members of the aristocracy whom they had been able to recognise in the audience. Mrs Bainsbury leaned across and whispered in her ear.

'Isn't it a shame about Mrs Cuthbertson. All the seats were sold, so she's having to sit behind us—that row is only for sale on the day of the performance, and even this morning she only managed to get the end seat. She won't be able to hear the contraltos properly at all, poor thing.'

Delia twisted sideways and saw Mrs Cuthbertson sitting stiffly at the end of the row which curved round behind the sopranos. She looked uncomfortably out of place, for all her neighbours appeared to be students.

'Yes, it's horrid for her, isn't it?' she said. 'By the way, Mrs Bainsbury, what is it that's wrong with the Old Man? Do you know?'

The secretary's face froze for a second. Then she said slowly: 'I did phone him up this afternoon to find out. I think it's something he'll soon be able to throw off.'

She obviously did not intend to elaborate, and at this moment they were distracted by the entry of the soloists. Owen came last, he bowed to the audience and repeated to them the apology for Evan Tredegar's absence. There was an unmistakable wave of disappointment, but it did not discourage the young conductor. As he turned to the orchestra, his arms outstretched, his expression was one of triumph and he was breathing fast with excitement. But his fingertips were steady and as the introduction started everyone in the hall—players, singers and listeners alike—came under his control. Delia allowed the music to sweep over her for a few minutes; she lost herself in its surge and only when the rest of the choir rose to its feet did she shake her shoulders a little and turn her concentration on to her score.

THE PERFORMANCE WENT WELL. Only one incident marred the first part, before the interval, and that, Delia decided, was unnecessarily created by Owen himself. John Southerley, looking even younger than usual at the piano, had a difficult passage to play supported by the drums, all the other instruments being silent. He played it superlatively well, in Delia's opinion, but the drummer was slow and there was a moment of raggedness. Owen tried hard with his hands to bring the two together; then suddenly, while still beating time as vigorously as was necessary, he leaned slightly towards John and said, 'Slower, damn you, slower.'

The words were not shouted, but in the perfect acoustics of the Festival Hall they were heard clearly by every member of the choir and orchestra—and probably by the broadcasting microphones as well, thought Delia, with a surge of pity for John. Perhaps the same idea had occurred to the pianist, for he flushed with anger and rose slightly in his seat for a moment, as if he were going to stand. But his fingers continued the hectic runs and he settled down again, playing more furiously than before, his head down; there was no longer any pretence that he was watching the movements of the conductor.

As the first part of the work ended, Delia whispered across to Shirley, 'I fancy Owen will be getting a visit from John in the interval, don't you?'

'Serve him right,' muttered Shirley. 'Let's get out of here and have a drink.'

They made their way to the bar and sipped their long, cool drinks appreciatively.

'Tell me about the Mass,' said Delia, searching for a subject to take Shirley away from her sulkiness. 'What do you think of it? What are the critics going to say about it tomorrow, quite apart from the way we perform it?'

'Looked at just as a musical work, I think it's a masterpiece,' Shirley said simply. 'It's the best thing the Old Man's ever produced—perhaps the greatest work of the century, so far. But if you look at the theology of the music, that's all wrong— or at least, very questionable. I wouldn't be at all surprised if we didn't raise a few letters of protest from musical clergymen.'

'What on earth do you mean by "the theology of the music"?' asked Delia in bewilderment.

'Well, it's a Mass, ostensibly, and the words are the words of the Mass. But the music doesn't illustrate the words. As I see it, the music is a sort of re-living of the last moments of a dying man. I may be wrong, but that seems to me to be the only inter- pretation. It starts peacefully; perhaps the man knows that he is dying, but he faces it calmly. Through the first part it becomes more and more turbulent; the pain is increasing until it is almost too great to bear. That's where we are now. In the second part we can imagine the man being soothed by the priest. He accepts the consolation and the pain; the fear is still there, there are questions, sudden protests, but on the whole the music becomes more and more peaceful again. Then, right at the end, the man dies. Did you stay to hear the orchestra play the last section this morning?'

Delia shook her head.

'Well, you'll be startled then. I'd read the full score, of course, but even so I nearly jumped out of my skin. It ends with a shriek of agony. The consolation has not, after all, been enough.'

'Well,' said Delia, taken aback. 'I don't know whether to

congratulate you on your musical insight or on your imagination. Still, I suppose we'd better get back now.'

They turned towards the door and almost knocked into John Southerley, who was hurrying into the bar. On his upper lip he wore a piece of sticking plaster.

'Oh dear,' said Delia. 'Has John walked into a door, or could he possibly have come too near to Owen's fist?'

Robert Stanley, who was standing nearby, answered her.

'Owen's fist, I'm afraid,' he said. 'But that appeared in self-defence. I've every sympathy with John, but in the interests of the music he should wait until the end of the performance before he tries to murder the conductor.'

Together they returned to the hall, where the soloists and conductor again followed. The audience quieted at once and the second part of the work began. This time there was no hitch at all, except for Delia personally. Halfway through the Hosanna she became aware that Mrs Bainsbury, while still singing, was staring across towards the doorway below and to the left of the choir. As soon as there was a pause in the soprano part, Delia followed the secretary's eyes. What she saw there surprised her so much that she lost her place: it was by then in the middle of a complicated run and she felt very foolish opening her mouth soundlessly until she could find a familiar note again. That was the trouble with this perfect hall, she could hardly hear the voices even of her neighbours; throughout the evening she had felt that she and one of the back violins were performing the work alone.

The Mass was nearly at its end. The last chorus was a high one for the sopranos. Delia began to feel very tired and was glad when they had finished at last and could sit down. She listened with interest as the orchestra played the last section alone. The music swirled and rose. Owen was throwing himself about now —too much, thought Delia, who preferred a more restrained form of conducting. Suddenly violins, flutes and organ shrieked upwards; the two trumpets joined them on their highest note and began to slither down in a despairing scale. Together they faded gradually away, leaving nothing but a forlorn, hopeless memory and a roll of drums. Owen turned sideways on his rostrum; he swung over towards the drummer, who sat almost in front of Delia, willing him on to an ever-faster movement. Then there was silence; in what seemed a continuation of the same movement Owen turned to face the audience, his back to the choir, his hands outstretched to grasp the sides of the rostrum.

For a moment Delia sat dazed. Although she had been warned, the primitive power of the last bar had startled and shocked her, and she suddenly felt the effect of the emotional strain of the whole evening. She looked with a half-smile at Mrs Bainsbury, who was sitting forward pale-faced, her fingers moving nervously. She felt Delia's eyes, and tried to smile back.

'I didn't know it would be like this,' the secretary whispered. She said more, but it was impossible to hear. For after little more than a second's silence the audience had risen to its feet and the sound of cheering would have drowned even the most powerful efforts of the choir and orchestra combined. Delia found herself gasping as wave upon wave of applause seemed to hit her in the face. She glanced up at Simon; he too was standing, and as she looked, he smiled at her and gave a specially soft token clap for her alone. To conceal her blush of pleasure she looked down and then, out of the corner of her eye, glanced to the left at the doorway; but there was no one there except a uniformed attendant.

'They oughtn't to, really,' said Shirley—almost shouting to make herself heard. 'After all, it *is* a Mass.'

'Well, since they *are* applauding,' Delia answered, 'I do think Owen might wave us all up to take a bit of it. He must be trying to set a record in long low bows.'

They both looked at Owen. He stood still as he had stood

when the Mass ended, facing the audience, with his hands gripping the sides of the conductor's rostrum and his head and shoulders bowed forward. As they watched, his head dropped still further, until it seemed to be hanging uncomfortably between his shoulders. Delia drew in a quick breath and at that moment John Southerley rose from the piano-stool. He thrust his way towards the rostrum, knocking over a violin stand on his way. Before he could reach the conductor, however, Owen's legs suddenly bent at the knees. His hands relaxed their grip and, before the startled eyes of the still cheering audience, he fell headfirst to the ground.

CHAPTER SIX

In the artists' room the members of the choir and orchestra jostled uneasily. At first, they had whispered excitedly amongst themselves but now they were beginning to tire of their wait; until they heard further news there was nothing more to be said. A few of the younger ones were still hoping that something might happen, but most were merely wondering whether they would soon be allowed to leave.

Of them all, Delia was the most unhappy. There had been a moment when she had felt great admiration for Simon, had been proud to know him. He had pushed his way through the members of the audience who were filing out in a silent embarrassment of helplessness and had joined the St. John Ambulance man who was already kneeling by Owen's head; at that moment he had seemed purposeful, efficient, in control. She had been glad that he was a man who knew what to do, who did not get flustered.

But now the admiration had been replaced by uneasiness. From the moment when Simon had disappeared, leaving Owen untouched on the floor with the ambulance man to keep away anyone who might try to move him, Delia had realised that the young conductor must be dead. She tried to persuade herself that a heart attack would be easily explained by the unusual excitement which Owen must have been feeling at that moment, but there was something in the grimness of Simon's face which made her doubtful. And Christmas was so near, and her evening had been so perfect; her first sincere sympathy for Owen had changed to a selfish feeling of resentment.

A door opened; through it Delia caught a glimpse of Simon replacing a telephone receiver. At the sight of the uniformed policeman who emerged, the crowded room was immediately silent, and he was able to make his announcement quietly.

'Superintendent Hudson wishes all members of the Managing Committee of the Metropolitana to remain behind. Everyone else may go, but will each of you please give your name and address to the police sergeant at the door, and will the leader of the orchestra and the secretary of the choir stand by the door to check that this is done correctly. Would Miss Jones come in here first, please.'

Everyone stared at Delia as she made her way towards the door which the police constable held open. He shut it behind her, and she was alone in the little office with Simon.

He rose to his feet as she entered and smiled at her gravely but made no attempt to touch her in any way. As she sat down and faced him across a desk she felt nervously as if she were being interviewed for a job, and her voice, when she spoke, did not seem to belong to her at all.

'Is Owen dead?'

Simon nodded. He too seemed a little nervous; his pen was drawing unconscious circles on the notepad in front of him.

'Naturally?'

'I'm afraid not. That's why I'm here. I've just been reporting to headquarters, they've told me to take over the case as I've been on the spot from the beginning. I'm sorry.'

He added the apology when he saw the unhappy expression

49

on her face. Then he took a deep breath; but he hesitated, and when he finally spoke, he was staring down at the desk.

'There's something I want to ask you.'

Delia laughed to herself bitterly. That was a sentence she had expected him to speak to her that evening—but at a table overlooking the lights of the river, not here; and with eyes tender and not grave.

'Owen Burr has been murdered. I want to know—and I'm asking you unofficially, so to speak—whether you know anything about the murder at all, whether you had anything to do with it.'

For a moment Delia could only stare at him, speechless with incredulity. She decided at last that he must after all be joking in some way and smiled at him feebly.

'What would you do if I said yes?'

'I should leave the case to the man who would have handled it if I hadn't happened to be here. It could probably be arranged without causing any comment.'

So it was not a joke. Slowly Delia rose to her feet.

'You mean that you are seriously asking me whether I had a hand in killing a man?'

'Please don't misunderstand me. I certainly don't think that you had. But I don't want to get deep into this investigation and then perhaps find out something that you might not want me to know.'

Delia looked at him stonily.

'Funny,' she said with a short laugh. 'Only a couple of hours ago I was thinking that you loved me.'

'You thought correctly,' said Simon, standing in his turn. 'And if you still think it now, you would still be correct. I love you very much, although this isn't a time when–'

'You must have a curious taste, to love someone whom you believe to be capable of murder.'

'I don't believe it for a minute, Delia. I only asked because —'

'You believe it sufficiently to think it worthwhile to ask. I do not, apparently, strike you as the sort of woman who would be quite *in*capable of murder.'

'There are very few people with physical courage who would be quite incapable of murder—in some, unusual, circumstances. Sooner or later I shall find out what the "circumstances" were in which Owen was involved, and then I shall find out who else was involved in them as well.'

'And you think it could be me. Thank you very much.' She turned to walk out of the room, but Simon stepped forward quickly and laid a hand on her arm.

'Listen just a moment, Delia. I've been tactless, and I'm sorry. But look at it this way. This isn't a murder committed in drunkenness, in a sudden fit of temper. Owen was shot dead, and since I don't imagine that many concertgoers carry pistols in their pockets, that means that somebody came to this particular concert with the deliberate intention of shooting him dead. I don't know yet who it was, but when I do know you may find that it is someone you know and like, someone whom you could never possibly suspect of murder.'

'That may be true of casual acquaintances, but if you love someone, you *know*.'

'Do you think that no murderer has ever been loved by someone who refused to believe him guilty?'

'Well, I should think that the "someone" was absolutely right to have faith.'

'Now you've moved from logic to ethics. As a man I agree with you,' Simon said quietly, 'but as a policeman I had to ask that question.'

'And yet if I had given the wrong answer, you would have ignored it.'

'Even if you had committed a dozen murders, I should still

love you,' he said. 'It's just that I should want to know if there were any questions that were better not asked.'

'There was one,' said Delia, 'and you've asked it.' Later, she knew, she would remember his voice as he told her that he loved her, but for the moment she was still bitterly hurt. Again she moved towards the door, but again he prevented her. This time his tone was business-like.

'I'm afraid there are one or two questions I'd like to ask you officially before you go.'

A little sulkily, she returned to her seat.

'I wonder if you remember, a couple of months ago, after a committee meeting once, you said to me that you thought that one of these days Owen would find himself murdered by one of the Committee, or words to that effect.'

'Oh, for heaven's sake,' said Delia, suddenly angry again. 'I was only joking—and I'm not sure I didn't say Owen would do the murdering, anyway.'

'Well, whichever way it was, I got the impression that there wasn't much love lost between him and the Committee, and now I need to know why. Before we start, let's look at this.'

He pushed across the table a plan of the performers' seating. The conductor's rostrum at the top had been marked in red; from it ran three sets of double lines, narrowly together at the rostrum but widening as they drew further from it. One funnel thus created ran straight down through the central woodwind and tenors, stopping before the organ. Another ran diagonally down to the right, including the two adult male soloists and the piano, a section of the strings, most of the sopranos and a few of the cheap public seats behind them. The third, diametrically opposite to the second, was drawn widening upwards in the diagram and to the left; most of the area included was gangway space, but there were also a few of the end seats in the two front rows, and it ended at the doorway. Delia stared at the plan without interest.

'I've already had a report from the doctor,' Simon explained. 'Owen was killed by a bullet that entered his body under the right shoulder-blade and made its way diagonally across to the heart. Unless I can find someone who heard the shot and can give an exact time, I have to consider three possibilities. If the shot was fired while he was taking his bow at the end of the work, facing the audience, it must have come from someone in this second area here, the one which included the sopranos of the choir. On the other hand, it's possible that he might have been shot in the second before he turned, while he was still facing the orchestra; if he'd just started to turn, he could have continued the movement before he collapsed. The third area, this short strip pointing towards the organ, is not a very likely one really, but I noticed that right at the end Owen spent a few seconds leaning over towards the drummer. If he'd been shot just at that second, it would probably have been done by one of your tenors. But, as I say, that's not very likely. The most probable time was when he had already turned to the audience, which means that I need to look closely at the sopranos. What I would like you to do is to tell me where the members of the Committee were sitting during the concert. Let's start with your chairman.'

'It's a woman,' said Delia, still speaking reluctantly. 'Mrs Cuthbertson. She's a contralto, but tonight she wasn't singing. She had an ordinary seat.'

'Where?'

Delia pointed to the end of the public row behind the sopranos and Simon drew a little box at the place; it was just inside the second funnel.

'Why wasn't she singing?' he asked casually. 'Sore throat or something?'

'Owen kicked her out at the practice this morning. She was making an awful noise, so he told her she couldn't be with the choir this evening. She was very upset about it.'

'And angry?'

'Yes. Wouldn't you be—in front of all those people?' Suddenly Delia noticed that while Simon's eyes were fixed on hers, his fingers were scribbling unseen notes, and she spoke indignantly. 'But not murderously angry, I don't mean, only hurt.'

He looked at her calmly.

'Tell me, of all the Committee, was there anyone who never quarrelled with Owen in any way?'

'Shi—' Just in time Delia remembered what Mrs Bainsbury had said about Owen's quarrel with Shirley that morning. She thought quickly, uncomfortably conscious that Simon had noticed her false start.

'I think on the whole I was the one who fought with him least, because I had least to do with him. I don't think he thought me musical enough to be worth arguing with, and, on the other hand, I didn't do much of which he actively disapproved. Apart from me, and the Old Man, of course, I think there was only Mackenzie Mortimer. They used to spar a lot, but Owen never turned those arguments into personal attacks, as he did with everyone else.'

'Right,' said Simon. 'Now, where were they all sitting?'

Delia pointed as she spoke the names. 'Shirley Marsden, me and Mrs Bainsbury all in the front row of the sopranos. Mackenzie Mortimer and Robert Stanley in the front row of the tenors. John Southerley at the piano.'

She looked at the drawing silently as Simon marked the places. John and the three women were all, like Mrs Cuthbertson, in the second funnel; the two men in the first.

'Now then, have any others of these had any recent dispute with Owen?'

Delia thought for a moment. She had heard about Shirley so indirectly that she decided not to mention it but to leave it to

Shirley herself to explain. The quarrel with John Southerley, on the other hand, had been so public that if she made no mention of it her silence might afterwards appear surprising. She referred to it briefly, her eyes on Simon's scribbling fingers.

'Last question,' said Simon. 'Did you notice anything unusual at any time during the concert—anything at all, whether it seems relevant or not?'

Delia thought without success.

'Every concert seems to be different from the last,' she said, 'and this one had quite a new atmosphere, because it was a special occasion and a different sort of audience. Even if I did see anything unusual, I probably shouldn't have realised that it was, if you see what I mean.'

'I see,' said Simon. 'That's all then, thank you very much, Delia.' They stood up together. 'Are you going to forgive me?'

Delia smiled wryly.

'I expect so. But just at the moment I'm still a little hurt.'

He moved closer, his hand touched her arm.

'I can see now that it was stupid, couldn't have done any good. You could help me a lot on this if you would, Delia, knowing all the background. I'd like to get it cleared up quickly and then we can forget all about it.'

He was close now and very still. But there was a knock on the door, and he moved quickly away as the police sergeant entered.

'They've all gone except the ones you wanted, sir.'

'Good,' said Simon. 'Well, Miss Jones can go too. I'd like to see Mr Mortimer next.'

That gentleman walked in smartly and nodded his head at Simon as he took a seat. Simon sat for a moment in silence, considering the man; almost certainly a regular officer in his youth, he decided.

'I'd like to ask you a few questions.'

'Of course, of course. Anything I can do to help.'

'Were you in the Army long, Mr. Mortimer?'

He looked faintly surprised but answered reasonably enough.

'Not as long as I would have wished. I went in in 1939, liked it, stayed on, but they wouldn't give me a permanent commission. Ten years and ten months altogether.'

Simon nodded and changed the subject.

'Tell me, do you think John Southerley was seriously annoyed with Owen Burr this evening?'

'I'm sure he was. He's a young fellow, all worked up for his first big concert and then someone shouts at him in the middle of it. The blow to the pride would come later, no doubt, but the immediate effect on the temperament must be devastating. And then afterwards he'd have time to think about other people hearing it and perhaps the broadcasting microphones catching it; it's enough to make anybody see red.'

'Why did Mr Burr do it then? Spite?'

'Oh no, I don't think so. There was a musical reason of a sort; it's just that you couldn't expect John to appreciate that at the time. I've been a tympanist myself, as an amateur, and I should guess that Mr Tredegar never has. He'd written some rolls and changes for the drums that simply couldn't be played at the speed he'd marked. John certainly wouldn't realise that, and perhaps Owen didn't at first, but he cottoned on in time, and then the only hope was to slow John down. I was watching them then. John had his head down as if he were playing a solo, it was all set to be a real mess. Owen had to do something to steady things. He probably didn't choose the best way—but then, just like John, *he* was a youngish fellow all worked up for his first big concert as well.'

'Tell me, Mr Mortimer,' said Simon, 'what sort of a man *was* Owen Burr?'

'He was a musician, Superintendent, first, middle and last, a musician. As long as the music was right, nothing else mattered. He seemed ruthless with people, but only because he hardly noticed them as individuals. Either they helped the music and he liked them, or they got in his way and he knocked them down. As a conductor he was first class. As a matter of fact, although not many people would admit it, Evan Tredegar could never have produced a performance even of his own work like the one young Owen did tonight. And Owen knew it, too—no false modesty there. But he wasn't one to harp on things. He would have forgotten that brush with John Southerley before he left the rostrum at the end of the Mass.'

'Perhaps,' said Simon. 'But would John Southerley have forgotten it equally quickly?'

The precise little man stared at him in bewilderment.

'Have I been getting this wrong?' he asked at last. 'I assumed that Owen had had a heart attack.'

'He was murdered,' said Simon. 'Did you keep any firearms when you left the Army?'

'None. Are you suggesting…'

'I'm suggesting nothing. Merely asking.'

They looked at each other across the table, Mackenzie assimilating the news, Simon summing him up.

'Right,' Simon said at last. 'Will you just confirm that this mark on my diagram shows your seat and then you can get home.'

As the door opened, he caught a glimpse of Delia speaking earnestly in the next room to Mrs Bainsbury. The secretary's name was the next on his list.

'Well, if you're going next, I'll be off,' said Delia to her. She picked up her bag and moved towards the door. Then she stopped and stood very still for a moment before turning back to Mrs Bainsbury.

'You know,' she said slowly, 'he asked me whether I'd noticed anything unusual, and I said No. But there was one rather surprising thing, wasn't there?'

The secretary's eyes flickered and then looked straight into hers.

'Nothing,' she said calmly, 'which could possibly be of any relevance to the present investigation.'

CHAPTER SEVEN

'I believe you're a widow, Mrs Bainsbury.'

She looked across at Simon unemotionally. 'My husband died sixteen years ago.'

'How long have you been the Metropolitana's secretary?'

'About thirteen years. Even before that I used to help quite a bit, addressing envelopes and that sort of thing, but it was difficult while my son was young.'

'So I expect you know a good deal about the members of the choir.'

She smiled faintly.

'As much as anyone else, I've no doubt.'

'What did you think of Owen Burr?'

'I didn't like him. But he's dead now.'

'Don't let that influence anything you want to say, Mrs Bainsbury. Why didn't you like him?'

She hesitated slightly.

'I don't know that I can put a finger on anything particular; it was just his manner. Before his time, the Metro used to be a friendly choir, but since he came on the scene there were quarrels all the time. And at practices he'd hurt people's feelings, picking on them. A good conductor knows how to make someone feel ashamed of a mistake without pointing him out by name to everyone else, but Owen could never let well alone.'

'I see. So you felt a kind of general disapproval of him. Did you ever have any more particular disagreements?'

'We had our arguments from time to time. But there was nothing personal in them, and I don't remember any serious ones during the last few months.'

'Now tell me, do you know of anyone else—anyone besides John Southerley—who had quarrelled with Mr. Burr recently?'

'Yes. Shirley Marsden.'

There had been no pause for consideration and Simon was taken by surprise.

'Oh. How do you know?'

'I heard them at it after the rehearsal this morning.'

'Do you know what the quarrel was about?'

'I'm afraid not. They were both talking at the same time—shouting, rather. It was something about dinner, but you'd better ask Shirley herself for the details.'

'Does anyone else know anything about it, do you think?'

'Not directly, I imagine. I mentioned it to Delia Jones, but not more than I've told you.'

Simon paused for a moment, wondering why Delia had not passed on the information. As if she had read his thoughts, Mrs Bainsbury continued to speak.

'She told me when she came out of here that she hadn't said anything to you because all her knowledge was third-hand. I think she mentioned it to me particularly so that I shouldn't think that you already knew about it from her. But of course it was only a lovers' quarrel, I expect. Owen and Shirley were always at each other's throats about something. They seemed to enjoy it.'

'Tell me something about your treasurer, Robert Stanley. What sort of a man is he?'

Mrs Bainsbury answered slowly.

'He's a friend of Evan Tredegar. He's been doing the job for about nine years now. I don't know that he's exceptionally good at it, but it's a thankless job and he seems to be careful and do what's needed without making many mistakes. I don't get on very well with figures myself.'

'How did he get on with Mr Burr?'

She spoke even more slowly now.

'There was—something—between them seven or eight years ago, when Owen first came on to the Committee. They never had much use for each other after that. I don't know what it was all about, though.'

'Right. Now would you just point to your place on this diagram?'

Mrs Bainsbury identified her seat casually enough but continued to stare at the plan.

'What do these three stripes mean?'

'Don't worry about them. Now for my last question. Did you see anything unusual or surprising at all during the performance tonight?'

Mrs Bainsbury stood up to go.

'Nothing,' she said calmly.

'Well, thank you very much, then. Would you ask Mrs Cuthbertson to come in next, please?'

The secretary hesitated.

'She was sitting in the audience, you know. She didn't come out here with us. In fact, most of the audience had left, hadn't they, before you realised that Owen was dead? John Southerley isn't out there either, if you're going through the Committee.'

'Miss Marsden in that case, if you would then, Mrs Bainsbury.'

She nodded and left. Shirley came into the room a moment later. Simon looked at her appraisingly. In his regard of Delia during the performance he had not failed to notice the glitter of the blonde beside her. At the moment, however, seen at close quarters, she made a less dazzling appearance. Although she still held her head very straight, the make-up on her face was smudged where she had dabbed at tears. She pointed to her place on Simon's diagram without speaking and then waited patiently for his questions.

'How long had you known Owen Burr, Miss Marsden?'

'About five years.'

'And you were a close friend of his?'

'We were going to be married.'

'Oh! Was your engagement a public one?'

'No. Owen wanted to keep it a secret, so we did. He never seemed in much of a hurry actually to get married, but he wanted to be sure that I'd be there when he did make up his mind. I didn't like it much.'

'Did you ever quarrel about it?'

'Not actually about that; we quarrelled about other things instead, but I think it was the strain. They never lasted long— the quarrels, I mean. He was very fond of me really, and I couldn't do without him, although now I suppose...'

She looked down at the floor, swallowing hard.

'I'm sorry to have to ask these questions, Miss Marsden. But do you mind telling me when you had your most recent quarrel?'

Her eyes suddenly filled with tears.

'That's the awful part of it. We had one today, and we hadn't made it up and now I never can.'

'What was it all about?' he asked gently.

'Oh, I was rather silly. Usually he takes me out to dinner before a concert like this, and often we have lunch and spend the afternoon together before it as well. He gets—he used to get —very nervous, and I could usually keep him fairly calm. Well, this was a bigger concert than he'd ever had before, and I expected that we'd do the same today and then I found that he was having lunch *and* dinner with somebody else and he hadn't told me. I was a bit disappointed, that was all; I lost my temper and he lost his too.'

'Who was the somebody else, then?'

'The contralto soloist. He seemed to know her quite well, though he'd never mentioned her to me. I suppose I was jealous.'

'There's nothing more you want to tell me about it?'

'I don't think there is anything more.'

'Then thank you for being so frank. Tell me, have you ever used firearms?'

'Yes. But only against rabbits in the wood at home. Why do you ask that?'

Simon watched as she worked it out.

'But he couldn't have been shot. There wasn't any noise.'

'There are silencers, you know. And it was a very noisy piece of music towards the end. Tell me, would the general public know about the ending? Has it been printed?'

'Yes, but not issued yet. A few of the critics saw it last week, but that's all. The choir and orchestra have been using single parts. Of course, anyone who was at the practice this morning would know what was coming—but most of the choir left before the end part was rehearsed, I think. I only remember Mrs Bainsbury and myself staying to the end with the orchestra.'

Simon made a note and then laid a selection of keys on the table. All except one were attached to a ring.

'Can you tell me anything about these keys, Miss Marsden? You may have seen Mr Burr use them.'

Without hesitating, Shirley identified all those on the keyring but over the unattached one she shook her head.

'He didn't carry that one about normally, I'm sure. I can't think what it would be for.'

'Thank you very much, Miss Marsden. Would you ask Mr Stanley to come in, please?'

Something in her eyes prevented him from saying that he

was sorry for her. He watched her reflectively as she left, then at once his mind switched to the next-comer. Would Robert Stanley describe the eight-year-old quarrel to which Mrs Bainsbury had alluded? Even if he did, what possible relevance could it have here today? Simon sighed to himself as the tenor entered the room.

The interview was short. Ten minutes later Robert Stanley was hurrying towards Waterloo Station, indignant and a little frightened, but unshaken in his declaration that he and Owen Burr had never been on anything but the best of terms. In the little office, Simon wearily picked up his papers: it was half-past twelve.

As he walked slowly down the darkened stairs, he seemed to hear the faint sound of music. At first, he smiled ruefully, thinking that his head was singing with tiredness. Then he stopped abruptly, for this was not imagination; it was the finale of Evan Tredegar's Mass in C Minor.

Quickly, stumbling past invisible chairs, he followed the sounds until he found himself at the open door of the Recital Room. There was no light, but he could see the shape of a grand piano thrown open and there was only one man who could be playing that music.

'Mr Southerley,' he called. 'Would you like to tell me where the light switches are?'

There was no answer. Perhaps the pianist, his head bent over the crashing chords and runs, had not heard; certainly he seemed startled when Simon reached him and put a hand on his shoulder.

'Practising?' asked Simon.

'No. Working off a bit of bad temper. Who are you? You don't look like a burglar or a nightwatchman.'

'I'm a policeman,' said Simon. 'I'd like to ask you a few questions.'

John left his seat and switched on the light. He had taken

off his stiff collar and his tie, untied, hung dispiritedly downwards. His face was that of a sulky but still attractive schoolboy.

'What are you in a bad temper about?' Simon asked quietly.

'Being deprived of the pleasure of giving Owen Burr a thrashing. I wanted to kill him, and he died on me first.'

'Owen Burr has been murdered, Mr Southerley. I think we had better talk about the matter calmly. You will forgive me if I guess that you have been drinking. Do you mind telling me when?'

'Since the end of the concert. Nothing else to do.'

'You didn't have anything earlier in the evening?'

'No. Couldn't. Drink goes to my fingers. Don't touch it usually.'

'Why did you want to thrash Owen Burr?'

'Weren't you at the concert? Didn't you hear what happened?' His head dropped heavily into his hands. Simon looked at him for a moment without speaking, mentally visualising that the pianist's seat fell within the second funnel of his diagram. When at last he did speak, it was with sharpness.

'Mr Southerley. Owen Burr was shot, and from a position which may have been very near your own. Can you give me any good reason why I shouldn't think that the shot was fired by yourself?'

'I can give you three thousand and one reasons.'

'I should like to hear them all.'

'Well, the one is that you need two hands to play the piano. At the end of that Mass I was having to work hard—there weren't any rests marked in the score for taking out pistols and firing them. Look at it this way. I was convinced that Owen was trying to make me mess things up and I was determined to make a success of it; it meant quite a lot to me, you know. I was concentrating for grim life on playing well. I wouldn't have spoiled it for the chance of killing that little twerp. If I'd wanted to shoot Owen, there would have been plenty of more convenient opportunities.'

'But at the moment when he was facing the audience and bowing, you would presumably have stopped playing.'

'That's where my three thousand reasons come in. I was one of the soloists, you know. It's reasonable to think that a good many of the three thousand people in the audience would have been looking at me at any particular moment.'

'Somebody took that risk, though.'

'It wouldn't be such a risk for anyone but a soloist.' Suddenly he straightened himself up and looked coolly and altogether soberly at Simon. 'Do I understand that you are accusing me of murder?'

Simon stood up wearily.

'I'm not accusing anyone of murder. All I know is that someone is a murderer in fact and several other people seem to be murderers in wishful thought. Goodnight, Mr Southerley. Don't run away.'

He noticed, as he left the Recital Room, that the playing did not begin again.

As he let himself out of the building he shivered with the cold. Then he stopped in surprise, for a lonely figure was sheltering under a flight of stairs, turning towards him at the sound of his footsteps.

'Is that Simon?'

'Yes? Why—Delia. What on earth are you doing here?'

He wanted to kiss her, to prove to himself that she had forgiven him and had come back to show her forgiveness. But he could feel that she was not ready for that and did no more than put his hand through her arm as they walked over to the car park.

'Have you found out who did it?' she asked.

'There's one who seems more likely than the others, but, as you say, most of these quarrels aren't the sort of thing which normal people commit murder for. And except for being musical, they all seem perfectly normal. The one I think might possibly...'

'Oh, I don't want to know,' said Delia hastily. 'I'd rather read it in the papers like everyone else. It would be horrid meeting someone and knowing he was under suspicion all the time.'

'Okay,' said Simon. 'But in that case, you mustn't discuss anything I say with anyone at all, because you won't know which are the really important things. Not a word about the three funnels, for example. I say, you *are* shivering. It must have been frightfully cold waiting.'

'Oh, I haven't been here long; I didn't even know whether you were still inside. All the doors were locked, and I tried phoning, but no one answered. I only stayed because your car was still here, and I didn't think you'd leave it. It's just that I was thinking on the way home and of course you're quite right that I ought to help if I can and to tell you things even if I don't know what they mean.'

She paused and he squeezed her arm encouragingly.

'Well, you asked me whether I'd seen anything surprising this evening. As a matter of fact I did, but I forgot it when I was talking to you and only remembered when Mackenzie was in with you. You know it was announced that Evan Tredegar couldn't conduct because he was ill in bed. Well, he may have been ill, but he wasn't in bed. About a quarter of an hour before the end I saw someone staring across at the door in a funny sort of way, so I stared too when I had a break and there was the Old Man. He was standing against the edge of the door so that no one in the audience would see him, but he was clear to me. Of course, I *ought* to have been looking at the conductor.'

Simon stopped dead.

'Which door?' he demanded.

'The one on the choir's left. The one that comes into your third funnel.'

CHAPTER EIGHT

Simon pulled towards him the file which already held an outline of the life of Owen Burr; someone had been working hard through the weekend. He read it with interest.

Owen Williams Burr, born in Llanberis, Wales, on January 10th, 1925. Mother, Emily Williams Burr, unmarried, died 1938. Father's name not known.

Education: Llanberis 1930-36. Conway Secondary School 1936-8. City of London 1938-43. Royal Navy 1943-4 (invalided out). Royal Academy of Music, 1944-6.

Career: Worked in office of county rural musical organiser in Yorkshire, 1946-7. Came to London 1948 and took post as assistant librarian, Royal United Orchestra, and was appointed assistant conductor of the Metropolitana Choir in 1951. He appears also to have undertaken casual literary jobs in the musical world: proof-reading for musical publishers and acting as editorial assistant in the production of two reference books of music. In 1952 he formed a chamber music group which built up a high reputation and in 1955 he began to do free-lance work for the BBC, training special choirs for particular effects.

Unmarried. No relations known.

Simon spoke into the house telephone.

'Sergeant Flint? Here a minute, please.'

The sergeant entered smartly.

'You've done very well to get all this so quickly. I've only two queries to raise. Do you know what was wrong with Burr? Why did the Navy let him go?'

'I haven't seen the document yet, sir. I only had it over the telephone this morning and I was told he suffered a collapsed lung as a result of double pneumonia. He spent two days in a lifeboat in the North Sea in December 1943.'

'Right. The other thing is his father. No hints at all?'

'Not from Somerset House, sir. But Llanberis is a smallish place. It should be possible to pick up some gossip on the spot. Would you like me to go down?'

'I'm afraid not,' said Simon, laughing. 'Sorry to disappoint you. I may have to go myself, but we'll see how things go today. I'm expecting Mr Evan Tredegar at any minute. Show him in as soon as he arrives. Oh, and find out who paid Owen Burr's fees at the City of London, and also make an appointment for me to see his bank manager before lunch. Give him an idea what it's all about. I was up at Burr's flat yesterday and couldn't find any record of his financial affairs except a current cheque-book.'

'Right you are, sir.' Sergeant Flint disappeared but returned within a few seconds. 'Mr Tredegar is here to see you.'

'Show him in.'

Simon rose as the Old Man entered; he studied his visitor as they shook hands. But there was nothing to be learned from the deeply lined face. The eyes were sunken beneath folds of dry skin and over them the lids seemed to be permanently half-closed. Tredegar sat in the chair offered and waited, without any reference to the recent tragedy, for Simon to begin.

'I've no doubt you can guess why I asked to see you, Mr. Tredegar. It was very good of you to offer to come up here.'

'Not at all, not at all. Shocking business. Great loss to music. Anything I can do to help?'

'How long had you known Mr Burr?'

'Since he was a boy. Heard him playing at a school concert. Cello, most unusual gift. Should have kept it up. I was a governor, encouraged the boy. Glad to give him a job with the Metro. Never regretted it.'

'What year was this, that you heard him play?'

'No good on dates, I'm afraid. Before the war, though—1938, perhaps, or early '39. Couldn't say exactly.'

'And you have always been on good terms with him?'

'Certainly. Certainly. Both musicians, mutual respect. He was difficult, of course, but I could see he was going to be one of the great conductors. Worth encouraging him.'

'You weren't ever jealous that in the future his reputation might become greater than your own?'

'Different spheres, Superintendent, different spheres. I create, Owen interpreted. No competition. No comparison.'

'Did you know anything about his private life?'

'You mean about Shirley?' The heavy lids flickered fully open for a second and Simon caught a surprising glimpse of twinkling grey eyes. 'Not more than anyone else. Owen never talked to people, no close friends. Nice girl, though. Clever.'

'So that you wouldn't know if Mr Burr had any enemies?'

'Almost everyone he ever met, Superintendent, almost everyone. Too much ambition and no tact. But not enemies in the sense of potential murderers.'

'When did you first know that he had been murdered?'

'Don't run out of questions easily, do you, Superintendent? Saturday night. Mrs Bainsbury telephoned to me after she'd seen you.'

'You didn't know before that?'

'No.'

'Are you a close friend of Mrs Bainsbury?'

'Can't stand the woman. But I've known her for thirty years and she likes finding excuses to disturb me. In this case, she seemed to feel that I ought to have an official report, secretary to conductor-in-chief.'

'It must have been a great blow to you,' said Simon carefully, 'that you were not well enough to conduct the concert on Saturday yourself. I hope you are quite well again now.'

The grey eyes opened fully and stared innocently at Simon across the table.

'Never was ill. Never felt better in my life.'

'That must have increased your disappointment at not hearing the first performance of your work.'

'Heard it perfectly, Superintendent, perfectly. Beautiful place for acoustics, the Festival Hall. Don't know why people bother to pay for expensive seats when you can hear just as well free from the doorways.'

The twinkle was back in the eyes once more. Evan Tredegar was enjoying the failure of Simon's little plot.

'But if you were present at the concert, you must surely have known about Mr Burr's death before Mrs Bainsbury phoned you.'

'Not a bit of it. Left before the end—the second the choir finished. Lingered on the stairs to hear the applause but didn't want to be seen when the audience came out. Owen was perfectly all right when I left.'

'Perhaps you'd explain then, Mr Tredegar, why you attended the concert without conducting it.'

'Wanted to give the lad his chance. Difficult making a career as a conductor you know, Superintendent, very difficult. No one will let you conduct a big concert until you've conducted a big concert. When you're at the top, everyone wants you, but no one helps you to start. As for attending, you wouldn't have expected me to stay away on an occasion like that, would you? But as I was supposed to be ill, I couldn't let any of the audience see me. Had to be very careful in the interval. Otherwise people might complain. Fraud.'

'I don't understand, though, why you shouldn't have allowed Mr Burr to be billed as the conductor all along.'

Evan Tredegar moved restlessly.

'If you don't understand, Superintendent, I can't explain it. You'll just have to take my word that there are people who'd come to hear me conducting who wouldn't stir an inch for Owen Burr because they'd never heard of him. *He's* had to get himself murdered to become a national celebrity.'

'Obviously you behaved very altruistically, Mr Tredegar.' Simon's fingers were fidgeting through the open file in front of him. 'Tell me, have you ever done any mountain-climbing?'

There was just a second in which the grey eyes looked startled before they were hooded by the white-lashed lids.

'Matter of fact, yes, when I was young. Not for years now, of course.'

'Where did you climb, chiefly?'

'Started out on the Alps as a young man. Declined through the Cairngorms, Lake District and Welsh highlands to the age of fifty-five and then took to climbing the stairs to my flat when I wanted exercise.'

'I suppose you've been up Snowdon in your time, then?'

'Hundreds of times. More or less born on the slopes.'

'I hadn't realised that. You don't happen to remember whether you were there in 1924, I suppose.'

'Quite possible. No memory for dates. But I kept on my mother's house there after she died. Went there for holidays as often as I could. Welshmen aren't like the Scots, you know, Superintendent; they like to go home. Especially when they've come from a poor family and done quite well for themselves.'

'Which side of Snowdon did you live? The Llanberis side?'

'That side, but the other end of the lake. All this relevant?'

'I don't expect so. I won't keep you any longer now, Mr Tredegar. If you think of anything about Mr Burr or about Saturday's performance that might give me a lead, I'd be very glad to hear about it. Thank you very much for giving up your time.'

Simon was left alone. He received with a sigh the news that Owen Burr had paid his own school fees by cheque from the age of thirteen and set off to see the bank manager, consoling himself with the prospect of lunch with Delia.

He was late and Delia, who had only the time allowed her by the architect for whom she worked, was already eating macaroni cheese. He ordered something more appetising for himself and began to talk at once.

'Well, I've seen your Old Man. He's put himself fairly well in the clear. He didn't make any secret of the fact that he'd been at the concert, although he said he left early.'

Delia's face showed her relief.

'I'm so glad. I didn't really think that he could be mixed up in it. It was about a quarter of an hour before the end that we saw him, I think. Certainly when I looked again after the work was finished, he'd gone.'

'Who do you mean by "we"?' asked Simon.

'Well, I suppose several people in the choir may have seen him, but it was after Mrs Bainsbury had been staring that I first noticed him.'

Simon put down his knife and fork.

'Does Mrs Bainsbury know that you saw him too?'

Delia thought hard, trying to remember.

'Yes, I think she does. I seem to remember saying something to her about it, though I'm not sure what it was. It was before I'd mentioned it to you, in fact. I'd only just remembered, and I wasn't sure whether or not it mattered.'

'But even if she thought then that I didn't know, she must

have realised that you would almost certainly discuss it with me sooner or later; I've called for you several times after Committee meetings at her house. She phoned the Old Man on Saturday night. Almost certainly she warned him then—so that innocent, forthcoming admission of his doesn't mean a thing after all. I'm just back where I started. Except that I've discovered one possibly interesting thing. Tell me, did you ever notice any resemblance between Owen and the Old Man?'

'They had the same hands,' Delia replied promptly. '*I* often noticed that—but perhaps most musicians have the same sort of hands. There was one other thing, too. They used to run their hands through their hair in the same way, except that Owen did it in a rush and the Old Man very slowly. But they were quite different to look at—with forty-five years' difference I suppose that's not surprising. Why do you ask?'

'I've got one more question first. Do you know anything about the Old Man's love life?'

'Simon! At the age of seventy-nine!'

'At any time. Even if it's only rumour.'

'Well, it certainly won't be anything else. I have heard that he was a bit of a one for the ladies once, as a matter of fact. Apparently, his wife—though Mrs Cuthbertson seemed a bit doubtful as to whether he married even her, though they lived together for years—died when he was fortyish and after that he never settled down again. You ought to ask Mrs Cuthbertson. She's known him for years, and she doesn't like him much. Now you must tell me what you're getting at.'

'Would it surprise you if I suggested that Owen Burr might have been the son of Evan Tredegar?'

From the look on Delia's face it was obvious that it would.

'Did he tell you that?' she gasped.

'No. I'm only guessing. But listen to this. The Old Man visits regularly that place where Owen was born. When he's thirteen, the boy's unmarried mother dies and he's promptly whisked away from a perfectly good school in Wales to London. As soon as he arrives, he begins to receive an allowance of £350 a year, out of which he pays his own school fees and £2 a week to a widow who looks after him. The £350 is paid into his account by Evan Tredegar, who has previously appeared to have no knowledge of his existence at all. It's fairly suggestive, isn't it?'

'Did the Old Man tell you all this?' asked Delia in astonishment.

'No indeed—though it's possible that he might if I asked him. I got most of it from Owen's bank manager. Anyway, if the Old Man *were* Owen's father, it would make it more understandable that he should have stood down to give his son his first big chance at the concert.'

'Is that what he said?' Delia asked doubtfully.

'Why, yes. What are you frowning about?'

'I'm not sure. It's just in the back of my mind. There was a telephone conversation I heard. It didn't mean anything at the time, and I can't remember what was said, but when I heard later what was happening it left me with a very definite impression—more definite than I'm being now, I'm afraid.'

'Never mind that. What was the impression?'

'That it was Owen who was ordering the Old Man to stay away.'

CHAPTER NINE

Simon stared at Delia.
'Are you sure of that?'
She shook her head.

'There's nothing I could swear to at all. I don't remember any exact words. It's just that after I heard that the Old Man wasn't coming, I suddenly had a feeling that he wanted to come but that Owen wouldn't let him. The feeling was more than just a guess; it was based on something I'd heard that I wasn't intended to hear.'

Simon sat so still that a nicely browned roast potato which he had been saving until last on his plate was whisked away by a silent waitress.

'Let's assume that Owen was the Old Man's son,' he said at last. 'And let's also assume that your feeling is quite correct, that Owen forced his father to stay away. Now, why?'

'So that he could get the Press notices, of course.'

'No, I mean why did the Old Man put up with it? Why didn't he simply say, "Go to hell"?'

This was a more difficult one and they both sat in silence for some minutes.

'Do you think Owen was the blackmailing type?' Simon asked suddenly.

Delia considered.

'I don't really know what blackmailing types are like,' she said. 'I don't think for money, but of course he was terribly ambitious. I suppose he might have used a threat of some sort to get himself a push-up.'

'Right. Then what's the Old Man's weak point—criminally weak point?'

'Well, Owen himself, his very existence.'

'It isn't criminal to have an illegitimate son.'

'Surely blackmailers don't restrict themselves to the use of criminal offences. People will pay to keep their reputations as well as their freedom, won't they? And look'—Delia was by now very excited with her theory—'you remember I told you there were rumours that he might be knighted at the New Year. Well, suppose the rumours were true, the Old Man wouldn't want all his old dirty linen dragged out just now, would he? It might be worth his while to keep Owen quiet for a couple of months.'

'The New Year Honours List will have been settled in the autumn. It isn't put together at the last minute.'

'Oh. Well, I didn't know that and perhaps the Old Man wouldn't either. Anyway, if a lot of scandal broke out about someone a fortnight before his knighthood was due to be announced, they might hold it up, mightn't they? It would look so bad otherwise.'

'You're very persuasive, but there's one snag. If the Old Man really thought this was something worth committing murder for—and I think I'm prepared to accept it as a motive, if it's true —then, surely, he would have killed Owen *before* the concert, so that he could conduct the Mass himself after all.'

They were both silent until Simon spoke again.

'Well, there are a lot of things to be checked. There are too many theories and not enough facts at present.'

'What sort of people *are* murderers?' asked Delia meditatively.

Simon laughed shortly.

'You don't really expect an answer to that question, do you? There are almost as many kinds of murderer as there are people who commit murder. The brutal type, the drunken type, the frightened type, the mad type and the type who becomes so worked up about some quite insignificant irritation that he becomes mad for a short time. The last sort are the most difficult to find, of course, because most of their friends think of them as completely normal. You have to have the key-word before you can unravel the code.'

'If it's one of that sort we're looking for, the music of the Mass might have helped him to get worked up as well—did you find it had any effect on you while you were listening?'

'Yes, I did,' said Simon, almost blushing. 'But I'm not going to tell you what it was. I'm prepared to grant you the point, however, that anyone already in an emotional state might find his emotions intensified by it.'

Delia smiled at him, understanding perfectly.

'In fact, I'm sure that the *time* when Owen was shot is the most important thing,' she said. 'A clever, sane man who had the choice would surely have done his murdering privately, at a time when there was nothing to connect him with Owen at all. Someone who was mad all the time, or so furiously angry that he had come to the concert especially to kill Owen, would probably not wait until the very last note. I'm sure there's a musical reason for the timing. It was either someone sane who wanted to hear the whole work, or someone not quite sane whose emotions were being whipped around and who therefore felt an emotional need to wait until the climax of the whipping. But oh dear,' she added, sighing, 'I suppose it could just as easily be someone quite different.'

'Would you consider John Southerley sane?'

'Simon!' she gasped. 'You can't think it was John. Was that what you meant on Saturday night? I'm sure John would never kill anyone.'

'As a matter of fact, he told me himself how much he had looked forward to polishing off Owen.'

'But not seriously, Simon. And anyway, a man who'd just killed someone wouldn't go around shouting that he had intended to do so.'

'He might if he were clever, hoping that I'd argue just as you have done.'

Delia sighed.

'This is all too complicated for me. But I'm sure John wasn't the murderer. If you suspect that he is, then I suppose I shall have to help you find out that you're wrong—even if it does mean that somebody else whom I like may be involved. Don't you hate being a detective, Simon?'

'Not as much as I hate the idea of murderers walking about loose. But I agree that it's not so pleasant when one's friends are involved. You'll be careful what you do though, won't you, darling?'

'Oh, I'm only going to ask a question. I'll give you a ring tonight. Now I'm late.'

She picked up her bag and left before Simon had time to free his chair. At a more leisurely pace, he paid a visit from which he discovered that Evan Tredegar had been notified a few weeks previously of his forthcoming knighthood. Much of the rest of the afternoon he spent on the telephone, delivering a string of questions to the police station at Llanberis.

It was the next morning before Delia phoned and by that time Simon had learned enough to make Owen's paternity almost certain.

'I've asked my question,' she announced at once.

'What was it, and of whom?'

'Of Shirley. When Owen's about to conduct a concert she usually spends the afternoon before it walking round London with him and keeping him calm. I asked her if she did that this Saturday and whether the Old Man would have known where to find them.'

'And the answer?'

'The answer was an explosion of tears. Apparently, Owen spent the whole afternoon with what's-her-name Badham—you know, the contralto soloist; Shirley didn't see him at all. But after she'd finished crying, she said that the Old Man phoned her three times during the afternoon, asking if she knew where he could get hold of Owen. The last time was at seven o'clock.'

'Mm. That's not really enough, Delia. It suggests that he couldn't have killed Owen between the rehearsal and the concert—but if he was going to do it at all, why not on the night before, or as soon as he knew he was to be kept away? It looks as though I shall have to pay the man an official visit.'

'To arrest him, do you mean?'

'Good heavens no. I haven't got anything solid enough to act on at all yet—and one needs a good deal of solidity before one starts accusing national figures of murder. Anyway, thanks for closing one door.'

He arrived at Evan Tredegar's flat unannounced; it was on the fourth floor of a luxury block in Twickenham. The door pushed open slightly beneath the force of his knock but was stayed after a few inches by a short length of chain. Simon examined the useless lock with interest; splinters of wood showed how it had been forced by a heavy blow from outside.

The maid who answered his knock was apologetic about the door.

'It was an accident on Saturday, and we haven't had time to get it mended yet; workmen are so slow, aren't they, sir? Did you want Mr Tredegar?'

'If you please. What happened on Saturday, then?'

'I don't know exactly, sir, because I don't come in at week-ends. But when Mr Tredegar got up in the morning, he found the mortice locked, which neither he nor I ever did, and his key vanished, and there's no fire escape here, you know, sir, though I do say there should be, on the fourth floor like this. Mr Tredegar had to send for the police or the firemen or somebody before he could get out. What name shall I say, sir?'

'Superintendent Hudson.'

'Oh, are you from the police too, sir? I'm sorry I didn't know. Will you come this way, please?'

He followed the girl into a study where Evan Tredegar was pasting Press notices into a large black album. The preliminaries over, Simon asked his most important question at once.

'Mr Tredegar, why did you not tell me yesterday that Owen Burr was your son?'

Closely though he watched, he found it impossible to tell whether the musician was startled. The reply was certainly smooth enough.

'Didn't see that it had any relevance to the matter you were investigating.'

'It had some relevance, surely, to the truthfulness of your answers.'

'Very little, you know, very little. Not a family man myself. Never had any sort of paternal relationship with Owen. Only met him on business.'

'Nevertheless, Mr Tredegar, I would appreciate it if you would answer any further questions of mine with the strictest accuracy and leave it to me to determine their relevancy.'

'You're impertinent, young man.'

Simon stifled the obvious retort.

'I'm sorry if I seem to be,' he said politely instead. 'I'm only trying to treat a serious matter seriously. Will you tell me, was he financially dependent on you?'

'Certainly not. Settled £10,000 on him ten years ago, but he earned a good enough packet himself one way and another.'

'So that as far as you know he was not short of money?'

'Had no right to be. Nothing to stop him drawing on the capital if he had a bad patch. Never discussed it with him.'

'Now, Mr Tredegar, when did you discover that you were not going to be allowed to conduct your Mass on Saturday?'

The Old Man looked for a moment surprised by the question, then appeared to understand its wording and nodded his head.

'See what you mean. Wondered at first. About half past eight on Saturday morning. Doctor was most firm about it. Great disappointment.'

'Your doctor certainly seems to be an early riser. I can never get mine to budge until he's finished *The Times* crossword over breakfast. Could I have the name and address?'

For the first time Tredegar appeared to be at a loss. The pause was too long, the answer too casual.

'Certainly. Edgar Smiles, Devonshire Mansions. But he didn't come round himself to see me on Saturday. Gave me instructions months ago that as soon as I had another twinge, I must lie down all day. Heart, you know. Nothing to be done; just rest and let it go.'

'I see,' said Simon. He pulled from his pocket the key which had not been attached to Owen's keyring. 'Do you recognise this key?'

'Where does it come from?'

'From Owen Burr's pocket.'

There was a long silence. Simon stood up briskly.

'With your permission, I'll just see whether it fits into your broken mortice lock.'

'You can wait until you're leaving. I think you will find that it does belong here. Was only wondering how it had come to be in Owen's pocket.'

'For the second time, Mr Tredegar, I must ask you to answer my questions frankly. When did Mr Burr last visit you?'

'On Friday evening. Went through the score together; he told me the various tempi to which the choir had been accustomed and there were a few changes of phrasing he had made.'

'All quite amicable?'

'Most, most.'

'And could he have taken the key with him when he left?'

'Quite possible. Must have done, in fact. He let himself out. Only use that particular key when I'm leaving the flat empty; keep it in the lobby.'

'That must have been when he helped himself, then. Now, Mr Tredegar, suppose we hear what really happened on Saturday morning. I think we can forget about the doctor, can't we? It was only yesterday that you were assuring me you had never felt better in your life.'

'Teasing you yesterday, teasing you. Knew you were hoping that I'd deny going to the Hall. But you can have the truth if you like.'

'I do like, Mr Tredegar,' Simon said heavily. Evan Tredegar shot at him under bushy white eyebrows the look of a schoolmaster for a naughty boy.

'Rehearsal was at nine on Saturday morning. Got up early, got myself breakfast—Annie doesn't come in at weekends. Put on my coat, walked to the front door and it wouldn't open. Note from Owen fastened to the lock, saying that he proposed to conduct the performance himself. Young blackguard. No other way out of the flat. Much too high.'

'So what did you do?'

'Phoned the scoundrel up at the Hall as soon as I could reach him. Threatened to make the whole thing public if he carried on with it. He didn't appear to worry—intended to make such a splash with that Mass—*my* Mass—that no one would care how he came by it.'

'Why didn't you phone the police?'

'I did later. But after I spoke to Owen, I had a heart attack. I really have got a heart, you know, not pulling your leg about that. Flat on the floor until one o'clock. Quite conscious but couldn't move. Not at all funny. All Owen's fault, damn him.'

'So you phoned the police and they came round and broke the door in. Why didn't you go down to the Hall and conduct the Mass that evening after all, since you were free?'

'Two reasons. For one thing, my heart still gave me a twinge whenever I moved my left arm; wasn't quite sure whether I could get through all right. For the other, it's dangerous conducting a concert when you haven't taken any rehearsals at all. Anything might happen. Wanted the Mass to be a success, you understand, and Owen had the better chance of making it so, thanks to his own devilry. But after it was over, I meant to ruin him—write to all the papers and all that. Can't do it now the boy's dead, of course.'

He looked straight across into the eyes of his interlocutor and Simon, taken by surprise, looked down at the notebook on his knee. He did not know what to think. After so many lies, why should he believe this version? Yet it sounded plausible enough; until he had consulted Dr Smiles, he had no means of testing its possible truth. He sighed slightly, hoping for some miraculous intervention, some solid discovery that would lift him outside all these paths of mere possibilities. None came, and he asked his next question without enthusiasm.

'Did anyone know that Owen was your son?'

'No.'

'Did Owen know himself?'

'He wasn't meant to. He may have guessed, from the fact that I made myself financially responsible for him after his mother's death. The story was that I was a close friend, a boyhood friend of his father, who died before he was born. But he had imagination. He may have realised the truth—never mentioned it to me, though.'

'Would you have objected if the truth *had* become known?'

'Never thought about it. Not something I should want to proclaim unnecessarily, of course. No need for it to come out now, is there, Superintendent—at the inquest, I mean? That would mean a lot of publicity, wouldn't it, with the fellow getting himself killed in those circumstances?'

'I'm afraid it might. I don't expect it need be mentioned at the inquest unless the coroner especially asks, but of course it may prove—relevant—later on. I may have to trouble you again in a day or two, Mr Tredegar, I'm afraid.'

The Old Man rose majestically.

'I shall be here. Sorry if I've held you up at all. Circumstances were rather unusual; wasn't quite sure where I was.'

'I'll show myself out,' Simon said as he shook hands.

'Annie will be there. Oh, but you want to try the key of course. Perhaps I can have it back when you've finished with it.'

SIMON SATISFIED himself that the key had been traced to its proper home before calling on Dr Smiles. After a long wait, punctuated by icy remarks from a receptionist who saw her whole programme of appointments for the day disrupted, he learned that Evan Tredegar was indeed under warning of the danger to his heart from over-exertion ('Though over-weight is the root of the trouble, Superintendent') and that Dr Smiles had in fact been called in on Saturday and had found his patient in a very dangerous state, the heart being in a state of over-stimulation. It was not possible to tell whether this came from physical effort or from some form of excitement. The time? He remembered it perfectly—a most inconvenient one. He had been sent for at twenty minutes before midnight.

CHAPTER TEN

'Delia will be down in a minute,' said Mr Jones later that
day. 'She is just arraying herself suitably. It is very kind
of you to drive her in to her committee meeting. Getting into
the centre of Town is simple from here, of course, but to go
from one outskirt to another can take hours. But you mustn't let
her use you as a taxi-driver.'

'I like to be used, thank you, sir,' Simon said politely. Mr
Jones was in fact only twelve years older than his visitor, but he
spoke to Simon as to an inexperienced young man of twenty
and this had the immediate effect of securing to himself the
deference more properly due to a septuagenarian. Nor was he
unaware of this, and at the moment he was bent on exploiting it.

'I hope you're not going to use her, though, Simon,' he
pursued solemnly.

'I beg your pardon?'

'As a detective, I mean. This business about Owen Burr is
most unfortunate and I consider it even more unfortunate that
you should have been assigned to the task of apprehending the
murderer. It must be tempting for you to draw on Delia's
knowledge, since she is bound to be personally acquainted with

many of the people concerned. I trust you will be able to resist the temptation.'

'I wouldn't dream of asking her to do anything to which she objected, of course. She has seemed quite anxious to help in any way she can—I mean, she has actually offered.'

'May I suggest that you should refuse the offer. It is always unwise, in my opinion, to mix business with pleasure, and at the moment her relationship with you seems to be one of pleasure. I may say that I am extremely glad to find that is so. So many of Delia's friends in the past have been what one might call lame ducks. It is a great relief to me that she should now have formed a friendship with someone who has a normal degree of self-confidence.'

Simon found himself extremely embarrassed by this turn in the conversation, but luckily it was clear that he was not expected to make any comment. Mr Jones pontificated on.

'That is one reason why you would be unwise to suggest, even indirectly, that you are not capable of managing your own professional affairs. There are other aspects, however. It seems to me possible that a conflict of loyalties might arise in her mind. I think there is little doubt that if the murderer proves to be a friend, or even a pleasant acquaintance of hers, and she has helped you in any way to trap him, she will find it very difficult to forgive herself and perhaps impossible to forgive you for involving her. We cannot all look at these things from a purely professional point of view.'

Once again Simon, to his great relief, was spared the difficulty of making a suitable reply, for Delia appeared at this moment. She was warmly dressed and although, as usual, she went hatless, a headphone of white angora was firmly clipped over her ears.

'You're very wise,' Simon congratulated her, wondering as he looked whether he could afford to buy her a really good fur coat for a wedding present. If ever there was a wedding, of course.

'It's icy outside. There's still time for a white Christmas, and it feels as though it may be on the way. Are you ready now?'

'At once.' She turned to her father. 'Not too late tonight, I hope, but don't wait up.'

She kissed him on the forehead and led the way out to the car. As soon as they were on their way she turned to Simon.

'Were you discussing me when I came down just then?'

Simon grinned.

'Discussing is not the right word. But it is true that your father was elaborating on the subject of you.'

'I do wish he wouldn't. He knows I hate it. When he was forty, he took up psychology in a big way and he's never been able to leave anyone alone since.'

'Does he just dabble, or does he really know something about it?'

'Psychology? I don't know, I'm afraid. He's got some sort of diploma, but of course that may not mean anything. Where normal people are concerned, he tends to rub them up the wrong way—but I have noticed once or twice that he has the knack of persuading unhappy people to talk to him.'

'I'm obviously happy, then,' said Simon. 'I can never get a word in edgeways. Does he know many of the Metro Committee?'

'He's met them all, casually. We have Committee parties every New Year and he's been as my guest two or three times.'

'He doesn't know any of them apart from that—more intimately?'

'Oh yes.' Delia stopped herself just as she was about to proceed and glanced across at Simon's face, but he was concentrating, for once, on his driving and did not notice. 'Let me see, in the Committee,' she said thoughtfully, in a tone less enthusiastic than that with which she had begun. 'Shirley and John, I think, are the only two who have ever been home; he must have met them there once or twice.'

'John Southerley?'

'Yes.'

'I didn't realise you were a particular friend of his.'

'I'm not.'

'He's just another of the young men who never quite got round to kissing you goodnight on the doorstep, is he?'

Delia made no reply to that, but after a little while she volunteered an explanation.

'He's got digs quite near home. He used to drive me to and from Committee meetings and practices—it's a frightful journey by bus, you know.'

'You certainly have your transport well organised,' said Simon. Delia glanced across at him again but continued to speak calmly.

'He offered chiefly because he wanted someone to talk to about Shirley,' she said. 'His parents are both dead and I think he's very lonely. He was still only twenty when I first knew him, and incredibly young for his age—except as a pianist, of course.'

'What do you mean about Shirley?' asked Simon.

'He fell for her at sight, with the dog-like devotion of a lifetime—can't you imagine the effect she can have on a very young man? She never had any use for anyone but Owen, though— Shirley's no flirt, though everyone who sees her assumes she must be. So poor John was left to pine alone. They're quite friendly now, but at that time I doubt if she knew he existed.'

'Why didn't you tell me all this before?' he demanded.

'You didn't ask me, and I didn't think it was relevant. Is it?'

Simon threw both hands up off the steering wheel.

'Relevant! Everyone keeps talking about relevancy. All I want to know is fact—unassorted, unsifted fact. *I'll* give it relevancy.'

At his side there was silence and his brief anger turned against himself as he realised what he had done. He drew the car abruptly to a halt and put his arm round Delia's shoulder.

'That was a damn' silly thing to say. Please forgive me, Delia.

You've been so helpful all the time and then I have to pitch into you like that. I don't deserve you ever to speak to me again, but do, please.'

Still Delia did not speak. Simon bent over further and kissed her on the lips. The kiss became a passionate one; he held her tightly, and, as he kissed, he longed desperately to ask her whether she would be his wife. To be safe with her, to have no more fear of these stupid hurts and silences; he could hardly restrain himself from speaking. But she sat unresponsively, only allowing herself passively to be kissed, forcing him to realise that of all possible times for proposing marriage this would be one of the worst. He was silent himself now, feeling a little foolish as he withdrew his arm and re-started the car.

'I'd better take your father's advice,' he said gloomily. 'I won't mention this wretched case to you again.'

Delia managed a half-smile.

'I wasn't feeling offended then,' she said quietly. 'I was only thinking that I don't want it to be John.'

'You've got your tenses wrong,' he answered. 'Whoever it is has been a murderer, not is to be.' But the flicker of jealousy was with him again and it was for his own sake as well as hers that he struggled for a change of subject.

It did not come easily. In fact, as soon as he had spoken, he realised that his mind had refused to be dragged from the case.

'There's certainly a class structure in soloists for these concerts of yours, isn't there? I was staggered by the difference in the fees you paid for the Mass. Fifteen guineas for the poor contralto, thirty-five for the bass and a hundred for the tenor. It's just a matter of supply and demand, is it?'

'We got the contralto cheaply because no one's ever heard of her. As for the tenor, we only paid him fifty, as a matter of fact, though he would have been worth more if we'd had it.'

'Only fifty? Are you quite sure? I saw the agent this morning and his secretary told me that the fee was a hundred guineas.'

'What were you seeing him about?'

'Just trying to find out whether any of the soloists had any possible link with Owen.'

'And had they?'

So they were back again. But it was she who was making the running and presumably she would stop when she wished.

'Not the bass or the tenor. I didn't ask the boy; one doesn't want to drag a twelve-year-old into a murder investigation unnecessarily. Anyway, he and the contralto were sitting at the wrong angle. And it doesn't seem very likely that any of the solo singers—without the protection of the piano which Southerley might have counted on—would risk taking a pot-shot in full view of the audience.'

'The contralto had some sort of link, didn't she?'

'Yes, but it was very much in her interest to keep Owen alive. She was hoping that he'd be able to get her more jobs in the future. She was quite frank about it. I don't think Shirley really had very much to worry about. But look, about this business of the tenor. I don't expect it means anything, but find out how much your treasurer admits to paying. If he says fifty, don't make any comment, but say I'd like to have a look at his accounts. It may be that the agent is lying to keep up Cassati's fee, but I'd like to sort it out.'

Simon swung across the road and pulled up outside Mrs Bainsbury's house, where the presence of three other cars pointed to the fact that Delia would not be the first arrival.

'I shall be in my office for about an hour,' he said. 'Will it be any good my calling for you then, or will you still be hard at it?'

'I should think that will be about right. This should be quite a short meeting. It's chiefly a formality, to find out how we've done financially and sanction payment of all the bills. But I expect there will be a lot of talk about Owen, in the circumstances. I feel very guilty, though, dragging you out of your way like this.'

'I like it,' said Simon. 'If you're prepared to be driven by me, then I love driving you. Anyway, if I'm early, perhaps someone will invite me to join in the beer.'

'They're all much too frightened of you,' she said, laughing. 'See you later, then.'

As usual Roger admitted her to the house and took her coat. He seemed tired and did not speak after he had greeted her. Delia glanced curiously at a large, though fading, bruise on his forehead. 'Have you been kicked by a horse or something?'

'By a goalkeeper actually. Rough types, these undergraduates. I'm still seeing stars.'

'I bet you are. Well, this is going to be an uncomfortable evening, isn't it? Is Shirley here?'

He nodded silently and she made her way into the drawing room, where four members of the Committee stood, restlessly. Delia's eyes went at once to Shirley. She had her back to the others, pretending to be absorbed in the contents of a bookcase. When she turned, Delia was shocked; she had never seen Shirley look dowdy before. She was wearing the same clothes, her face and hair had been as carefully groomed as usual, but her eyes were dead and her lips unsmiling. Delia could think of nothing to say.

Robert Stanley and Mackenzie Mortimer were also there, fidgeting with papers and occasionally whispering to Mrs Cuthbertson. Mrs Bainsbury came into the room and distributed agendas.

'I don't think there's anyone else to come, is there?' she murmured to the chairwoman. 'Oh yes, John Southerley.'

His knock was heard at that moment. The Committee settled down into its chairs. While Mrs Bainsbury read the Minutes in her usual expressionless voice, Delia studied the agenda with some surprise.

'Election of chairman,' announced that lady. 'As I have resigned from membership of the choir, I am obviously no longer eligible to be a member of this Committee. May I have nominations for a chairman to take over until the end of the season?'

'But Mrs Cuthbertson,' protested John Southerley, 'is it really necessary for you to resign? I'm sure everyone here would be most sorry to see you go.'

'It was made fairly obvious last Saturday that my membership could be dispensed with. I do not propose to wait until I am snubbed again.'

Delia gazed at her incredulously. It hardly seemed possible that Owen's death could be ignored as completely as this; rarely before had Mrs Cuthbertson managed to express her feelings so strongly. There was no further comment. Mackenzie Mortimer was elected chairman and Mrs Cuthbertson, pursued by bewildered thanks and good wishes, swept out of the room and the house.

Mortimer requested the secretary to write a letter of appreciation to the ex-chairman and settled down efficiently to the management of the meeting. The treasurer reported a handsome profit on the concert, but nobody liked to show the cheerfulness with which such an announcement was usually greeted. He hurried through the list of payments to be authorised; Delia noticed that Cassati's fee was entered as fifty guineas but made no immediate comment.

'While we're on the subject of accounts,' she said casually just as Mortimer was about to move on to the next item. 'Superintendent Hudson has sent a message through me; he would very much like to inspect the Metro's accounts for the past eight years. I don't know whether the Committee's permission is necessary for that sort of thing.'

'If it is, I see no objection to giving it,' said the chairman briskly. 'I'm sure we would all like to help the Superintendent as much as possible.'

Shirley and John nodded in agreement. Delia looked across at Robert Stanley, who sat stiffly in his seat.

'I shall be seeing him after the meeting tonight,' she said. 'If you could let me have the accounts, I'll hand them over to him at once.'

The treasurer's face lost its final drop of colour.

'I'll have to send them,' he said hastily. 'I haven't them with me.'

'But that book you've been reading from,' began Delia.

'Not the right one at all. These are just the day-to-day items of expenditure and income. What Superintendent Hudson will want is the set of annual audited accounts.'

Delia looked doubtful but Mackenzie Mortimer, assuring her the Superintendent was not likely to mind a delay of one day, swept on through the agenda.

'Appointment of assistant conductor,' he read. 'Well, of course, we are all very sorry that this has to be discussed. I imagine we all want the secretary to record in the Minutes our most deep regret at the tragic happening last Saturday. Unfortunately, there is nothing else we can do, except for an idea of my own which I shall mention under Any Other Business. It is not pleasant to have to discuss the question of Owen Burr's successor so soon, but unfortunately, whatever our sentiments, we must remember that we have another concert in February and that the choir will be meeting again in a fortnight's time. It will be necessary to find someone to take over the work as soon as possible.'

'We can't settle much without the Old Man though, surely,' said John. He looked at Mrs Bainsbury. 'Do you think he will turn up later?'

She shook her head. 'He sent an apology. He is flying to Italy at ten-thirty this evening. A most inconvenient time to travel, but the arrangements were made at short notice and apparently it was the best that could be arranged. He did not mention when he expected to return. So I think we ought to make at least a temporary choice ourselves.'

Delia glanced at her watch; it was twenty to ten. The need to think quickly seemed to paralyse her brain. She turned to the secretary.

'May I use your telephone, Mrs Bainsbury?'

'Of course,' replied the secretary, looking puzzled. 'But— surely it can wait until the end of the meeting.'

'Yes, Miss Jones,' said the chairman. 'We still have some business to attend to.'

Everyone was looking at her with slight disapproval, but Delia's blush was caused by her sudden realisation that she was about to become an informer. She felt it necessary to her pride that she should act publicly.

'I think it may be urgent,' she said jerkily. 'Unless of course you think that the police already know that the Old Man is proposing to leave the country.'

'The police!' Mrs Bainsbury jumped to her feet, her notebook slithering to the ground. 'Why should the police be interested in Evan's movements? Why, he wasn't even at the Hall on Saturday.'

'But he was, Mrs Bainsbury. You saw him there yourself.'

'I deny that absolutely. In any case, I think it despicable that you should be acting as a spy. None of this is your business, nor that of the police. I will not allow you to use my telephone for this purpose.'

Mackenzie Mortimer intervened in an attempt to control the quarrel.

'We must remember that Miss Jones is a friend of Superintendent Hudson,' he said soothingly. 'Perhaps she knows more about the investigation than she is prepared or able to tell us. In any case, I don't see how any of us can object to the police learning information which I feel sure Mr Tredegar did not intend as a secret; they will doubtless decide themselves whether it is of any value.'

Mrs Bainsbury's hands were clenched tightly as she turned towards Delia.

'Do they suspect Evan, then? Are they going to arrest him?'

'I don't know, Mrs Bainsbury. I honestly don't know.'

She hated herself as she moved out through the silent room into the hall and dialled Simon's number with miserable fingers. She gave him the information without comment, noticing as she did so that the door of the drawing-room was ajar and that no sound came from inside it.

'What are you going to do?' she asked.

There was a silence.

'I don't know,' he said at last. 'I'm not ready to do anything. If he's got no reason for going, I can ask him to stay, but of course he will have a reason, and I can't see that I've got a strong enough case to make an arrest. I think my only chance is to drop a hint to Interpol and hope that the fact that he's so well-known will prevent him from disappearing. I'll drive down to the airport anyway—afraid that means I shan't be able to pick you up after all. Thank you for phoning. I'll let you know what happens.'

He rang off abruptly and Delia returned to her meeting. She sat unhappily to the end, approving without enthusiasm the new chairman's suggestion that a repeat performance of the Mass should be given as a special tribute to Owen. When the business was concluded she did not wait to share the refreshments but set out at once for home.

It was a long walk to the nearest convenient bus route, but she had not gone very far before she heard a car pull up beside her. John Southerley opened an inviting door.

'Going my way, miss?'

She accepted gratefully and seated herself beside him.

'Not often I have the pleasure nowadays. Boyfriend busy?'

'Mm.' She did not want to discuss it anymore and changed the subject quickly. 'What a wonderful coat you're wearing. It must keep you very warm.'

'As burnt toast. A posthumous present from my great-grand-father—a family heirloom, in fact. Stands up well to its eighty years, doesn't it? The only trouble is that it was built for a man with a considerably larger stomach line than mine. However, I hope to grow into it before I die.'

She stroked the curly black wool admiringly.

'I think it's magnificent. What is it—astrakhan?'

'That sort of thing, but slightly different. It weighs a ton, though. I can't imagine any little lamb skipping gaily about with this on its back.'

They drove along in silence for a while. Delia asked for a cigarette.

'Help yourself. Left-hand pocket of great-grandfather. The lighter may be there or else just in front of you. Light one for me, will you?'

Delia dug into the voluminous pocket and extracted two cigarettes from the packet she found there. Her hand returned for the lighter. The metal was cold, and she raised it straight to her lips. Suddenly she saw what she was holding and dropped it on to her lap with a quick intake of breath. John looked at her in surprise.

'Can't you find the lighter?' he said. 'Try on the tray, next to the duster. Put it back in my pocket when you've used it, will you?'

Delia's fingers trembled as she lit the two cigarettes. For a moment she sat in silence, her forehead wrinkled. Then trying hard not to let the two metal objects clink together, she returned to the pocket of John's great-grandfather the cigarette-lighter and the cold, murderous pistol.

CHAPTER ELEVEN

As the car sped along the road to London Airport, Simon wondered for the tenth time what he was going to do when he arrived there. The case against Evan Tredegar was so plausible, yet so incomplete. There was a motive of a sort, an opportunity which, although unsatisfactory, was no worse than that which anyone else committing the murder would have had to seize. It was not enough, but would he ever have anything more?

Yet he was afraid of being distracted by the obvious. With so many people who admitted to disliking Owen, it was easy to forget those other anonymous figures who might also have grudges, their personal hatreds. The untraceable groups in the front two rows, for example; he had no right to forget them, but how could he find them? He sighed, and then straightened himself as the car slowed to pass through the boundary of the airport.

'You'd better come with me,' he said to the sergeant who had driven him. 'And have your notebook prominent. I want to make this as official as possible; I think we'll frighten him a little. Go and fix a private room, will you, and then find me in the passengers' lounge.'

It seemed that Evan Tredegar had not yet arrived. The time which Delia had passed on to Simon was, he discovered, that at which passengers should report at the airfield; the departure of the plane was not until half an hour later. He glanced at his watch and was pleased; there would be plenty of time for a quiet talk.

Evan Tredegar caught sight of the detective as soon as he emerged from the passport control room ten minutes later. He nodded slightly in recognition, then moved towards a seat.

Simon came quietly to his side.

'Good evening,' he said.

'Evening,' replied the Old Man, surprised but not alarmed. 'What are you doing here? Just popping off for Christmas or waiting to catch smugglers?'

'Waiting to have a talk with you as a matter of fact, Mr Tredegar.'

'You'll have to wait a little longer then, I've no time now. Be back in England on Thursday.'

'I'm afraid my business is urgent. There's a room we can use over here, if you'd care to follow me.'

Evan Tredegar stared at him for a moment, then pulled a watch out of his pocket and studied it.

'Very well, then; five minutes,' he grunted. He followed Simon into the office and looked uneasily at Sergeant Flint, who was sitting in a corner but not unobtrusively.

'Now then, what's all this about?' he demanded.

'Do you mind telling me, Mr. Tredegar, why when I saw you this afternoon you made no mention of the fact that you proposed to leave the country.'

'Because I didn't know then that I proposed to leave the country; was only asked three hours ago. Damned if I see what business it is of yours, though.'

'Perhaps if you considered it for a moment, Mr Tredegar, you might think of a reason why we should be interested.'

The old musician considered and thought.

'Good God!' he spluttered. 'You're not suspecting me of killing Owen, are you?'

'Would it be so ridiculous if we did, Mr Tredegar?'

'Of course it would. Absolutely absurd. Why the devil should I do a damn fool thing like that?' He stopped and stared at Simon, then spoke more quietly. 'Am I to understand, Superintendent, that you propose to arrest me? If you do, I think you may find that you have taken on quite a lot of trouble.'

'If I did, I should not be deterred by any threats of yours. But as long as you can give me a satisfactory explanation of your very sudden departure, no, I do not propose to arrest you. I have no adequate grounds for doing so. But I *have* got grounds for suspicion and if you think back over what you have told me in the past few days and compare it with the truth, I think you will realise what they are. I am only saying this because I feel you may not realise the gravity of your position. It is more important than I can possibly emphasise that you should tell me not only nothing but the truth, but also the whole truth.'

He paused for a moment to let this receive proper consideration, then indicated a chair and nodded to Flint. When they were both seated, he began his questioning.

'Now will you tell me the whole story about this flight to Italy.'

'Certainly. Nothing to hide'—but the Old Man's voice was more subdued now, nevertheless, than in previous conversations. 'Had a phone call from the manager of the Rome Opera House at about seven o'clock this evening. They're putting on one of my operas tomorrow night—thing I wrote when I was thirty called *Oliver Cromwell*—hasn't been done in England for twenty years and quite right too. Anyway Fiorentino, who was to conduct it, is down with appendicitis and no one else knows anything about it. Would I come out and conduct the one performance, fat fee and all expenses paid? Said yes, of course. Have to be there for a rehearsal at three tomorrow afternoon; this was the only flight with a free seat. That's all. Booked to come back on Thursday afternoon, so shan't be out of your clutches long.'

'Can you give me the name and telephone number of the manager in Rome?'

Rather sulkily they were produced. Simon turned to Sergeant Flint.

'Call that number, or get an interpreter to do it for you, and check up. No scandal, though—you can be a reporter looking for a paragraph. I would like to suggest to you, Mr Tredegar,' he went on when the sergeant had left the room, 'that the reason why you did not conduct the Mass last Saturday was because Owen, your son, was blackmailing you.'

'Ridiculous suggestion. Nothing of the sort. Told you what happened last Saturday.'

'So you deny that absolutely, after careful thought?'

'Absolutely.'

There was an uncomfortable silence. Simon realised that Tredegar was trying to persuade himself to say something. He waited and it finally emerged.

'One thing I perhaps ought to tell you, though I suppose it won't look too good. Thought of it after you'd gone this afternoon. Insurance on Owen's life.'

'What about the insurance? You mean that you are the beneficiary?'

'Yes. Took out the policy myself, nothing to do with Owen.'

'For what amount?'

'Ten thousand.'

Simon whistled softly and an explanation was quickly forthcoming.

'Told you I'd settled ten thousand on Owen myself—absolutely, couldn't get it back. Well, Owen might die unmarried and intestate, no relations, but I couldn't claim—wouldn't want to, at least. Seemed a bit of a waste, so I took out this policy at the same time—about ten years ago—as a possible recompense. Thought you ought to know. Owen knew the policy existed, of course; he had to have the medical examination for it as a condition of receiving the money. But he didn't know that I was the beneficiary.'

Sergeant Flint returned and confirmed that the invitation to Rome was a genuine one and that a return seat had been booked. Simon held out his hand.

'I won't keep you any longer then, Mr Tredegar. Perhaps you'd give me a ring when you get back.'

The old man took his hand and shook it slowly. At the door he halted for a second and looked back.

'Didn't kill him, you know. Don't expect you to take my word, but I hope you'll get on the right track soon.'

He went heavily out. Simon looked at Sergeant Flint and shrugged his shoulders. They drove back to London in silence.

The next day and a half, to his extreme irritation, Simon was forced to spend in the Old Bailey, where two cases in which he was needed to give evidence had come up for trial at the same time.

When he finally arrived at his desk on Thursday morning it was to find a queue of matters awaiting his attention. The telephone rang while he was considering where to start. He listened without speaking for a few moments, expressed his thanks and rang off.

'That was from the Llanberis police,' he told Sergeant Flint. 'One of their men has just remembered that a young man was wandering about in the district only a few weeks ago, asking exactly the same questions that I asked them. Nobody seems to have recognised him, but the description would fit pretty well with that of Owen Burr.'

'Suggesting that he recently found out enough to make life awkward for his father?'

'Suggesting exactly that. Anyway, I'd better get on.'

'There's a Mr Southerley to see you, sir. He's been waiting some time.'

'Right. Show him in.'

John's face was pale as he sat down. Without speaking, he took from the pocket of his heavy black coat an object wrapped in a large handkerchief. He laid it on the desk.

'I wrapped it up in case there should be any finger-prints,' he said. 'There will be one set of my left hand, of course.'

Simon opened the corners of the handkerchief and stared at the pistol which lay there. Before making any comment, he rang for Sergeant Flint.

'Get this tested for finger-prints,' he ordered. 'Then take it down to Ballistics for a report, with special reference to the bullet which killed Owen Burr. Do you mind letting us have a set of your finger-prints, Mr Southerley?' he added.

'Not at all. I expected it.'

'Arrange that then as well, Sergeant. Now Mr Southerley, what's all this about?'

'I don't really know. I found this in the pocket of my coat this morning. It isn't mine. I can't think how it got there.'

They were interrupted while John's fingerprints were taken. Then Simon continued:

'How long do you think it's been there?'

'I've no idea. I hardly use that pocket at all. I had some cigarettes there, but I keep some more in my jacket pocket, and I don't usually smoke out of doors. I can't even remember when I last felt there—oh, yes I can, though. I remember smoking in the car on the way to the concert on Saturday; I was nervy. It wasn't there then.'

'Surely you would notice the extra weight as soon as it appeared.'

'The coat weighs a ton by itself; that little bit wouldn't make much difference. I did notice some drag last night but I thought it was caused by my cigarette-lighter.'

'Are you left-handed, Mr. Southerley?'

'No.'

'Have you had any experience with fire-arms?'

'Only as much as any National Serviceman.'

'Could you give me a list of all the public places in which you have left this coat since you lit your cigarette on Saturday?'

'I think so. I shared a cloakroom for the concert with Cassati and Wenski and the kid—that was at the Hall. Nothing on Sunday. The cloakroom at Drury Lane on Monday. A peg at Joe Lyons at lunch yesterday. Oh, and the hall of Mrs Bainsbury's house on Tuesday evening.'

'That was the committee meeting, of course. Did anyone arrive after you or leave before?'

'I was the last to arrive, but Delia left before me. She might not be alone in the hall though; Roger usually appears at the end of the meeting to sort out coats and open the door. Oh, and Mrs Cuthbertson left early, too; Roger probably didn't see her out.'

'And you came here as soon as you found this, Mr Southerley?'

'Certainly I did; it's all a bit mysterious, isn't it? I mean to say, it isn't mine and people don't leave this sort of thing around by mistake. I'm only too glad to be rid of it.'

'Well, thank you very much. There's not much I can do until I get the report up. There's nothing else you want to tell me, I suppose?'

John looked surprised.

'No, I don't think so. Should there be?'

'One always hopes. Right you are then, Mr Southerley. Let me know if anything else turns up.'

Simon waited impatiently for a few minutes, then went down himself to see what evidence the pistol would yield. The

Ballistics report was decisive; this was the instrument of the murder.

From the finger-printing department came, as he expected a print of the thumb and two fingers of John Southerley's left hand; as he did not expect, there was also another blurred set of a right hand. He stared at it without inspiration and sent someone out with the addresses of all the soloists and commit-tee-members, to collect specimens.

After a promising, if late, start, the day seemed to dry up. His phone calls with increasing frequency went unanswered until he remembered in surprise that it was Christmas Eve. Suddenly he felt tired and miserable. He rang Delia at her office.

'Simon here. I'm lonely. Are you free this evening?'

'As a matter of fact, and as usual, I am. What are you proposing to do?'

'Well, nothing, if you don't mind very much, since I'm even more tired than lonely. But I thought we might get dinner together at my flat and sit by the fire and murmur sweet noth-ings into each other's ear. Or does that sound too dull?'

'It sounds delightful. I'll let Dad know. Shall I come round straight from work? I expect we shall knock off early.'

'Good, then make it tea as well. I don't see why even a poor policeman shouldn't play hookey sometimes. I'll be there to open the door at half-past four.'

For the last hour he read over all the notes he had made on the case. They led nowhere, except to the conclusion that there was no reason why he should not take a proper Christmas holiday for once. Friday, Saturday, Sunday—it was a wonderful prospect, and he could see nothing at all which would be the worse for waiting until Monday. He locked his desk and went home.

THE LONG EVENING seemed to fly past. Delia settled herself on the floor in front of the flickering fire while Simon watched her happily from his chair. Although she behaved easily with him, there was still the slight restraint in her eyes which reminded him that he had hurt her, but he no longer allowed himself to be worried by this; he was going to get the whole question of Owen's murder well out of the way and give her time to forget it before he told her of his feelings. They did not speak very often.

'Did you have your finger-prints taken this afternoon?' he asked casually.

'No. Oh, have I missed something by leaving the office too soon? I hope your man won't try at home. Dad would be alarmed.'

'It's nothing very urgent—just that we've found the pistol.'

He described John Southerley's visit and Delia laughed up into his face.

'Then the prints will be mine—but please, that doesn't mean I done it.'

In her turn she described how she had found the pistol in John's pocket and returned it.

'But why didn't you tell me at once?' demanded Simon irritably.

'I thought it would be better for John to tell you himself without being asked. Then if he didn't say anything, it would mean something more definite.'

He was not quite sure whether to believe her, but she did not give him time to consider.

'Would you mind very much if we had the wireless on?' she asked. 'There's a big do on at Covent Garden tonight and I'd quite like to listen.'

He switched it on and turned off the light. For five minutes they listened to descriptions of the flowers in the Royal Box, the hand-painted programmes, the dress worn by the visiting Royalty for whose sake London society had suddenly discovered an interest in music. At last the opera, *Don Giovanni*, began and Delia settled herself more comfortably on the floor, her head resting against Simon's knee. She was soon absorbed in the performance, but Simon could hear little but the thumping of his heart as timidly he stroked her hair.

'He's too fat for it,' Delia said scornfully as Cassati's first notes were heard, but soon she had fallen once again under the spell of his voice, resenting the intervals. At the end she burrowed her head still more tightly against Simon's leg.

'You'd expect that a man would *have* to be nice with a voice like that, wouldn't you? I wonder what he's really like.'

'Probably very selfish and conceited,' Simon answered spitefully, aware that Delia would not stay with him very much longer. She rose to go at that moment, but first she had something to say.

'Are you not going to your brother for Christmas this year?'

He shook his head.

'I didn't know in time that I could get away. And it's a long journey just for three days.'

'Then you must have dinner with us tomorrow. We'd like it very much. We shall have it in the middle of the day, but don't come too early because I shall be busy in the kitchen until one. It isn't a turkey, I'm afraid, but it's an enormous goose, and I should hate to think of you being all on your own. Will you come?'

He kissed her and kissed her again.

'I'll be there at one, unbreakfasted and ravenous,' he said. 'Bless you.'

HE WAS punctual next day and the meal, although later than scheduled, was good. It was three o'clock before they sat down to coffee, and the telephone rang while the two men were cutting their Christmas cigars.

'It's for you,' said Delia to Simon. He took it unwillingly.

'It will be the office, I'm afraid. I had to give them your address in case anything urgent turned up. Hello. Yes. Oh, hello, Bill. Who have you lost today?'

'This may be nothing to do with you at all,' said Bill. 'But it concerns one of the people who was in on your show last Saturday, so we thought you might like to know. Ever heard of a bloke called Luigi Cassati? Well, he's just been officially registered as a Missing Person. He vanished into a fat piece of thin air at a quarter to midnight last night.'

CHAPTER TWELVE

'I'm going to finish this cigar,' said Simon. 'And then I suppose I shall have to do something; something highly intelligent and probably energetic as well. And after that excellent meal, all I really want to do is sleep. Pity the poor policeman. Will you please oblige me by keeping up a brisk conversation so that I have to keep awake?'

'On what subject would you prefer us to converse?' asked Mr Jones, stretching himself in front of the fire. 'The climate, or Signor Cassati?'

'Cassati, I think. Why should an eminent Italian singer disappear in England? Any suggestions?'

'Perhaps he's committed some horrible crime in Italy and doesn't want to go back,' suggested Delia.

'Is it possible that his disappearance is purely of a temporary nature—some young lady to whom he is attracted, perhaps— and that he is not aware that his absence has been missed?'

'Or perhaps,' Delia followed up her own thoughts, 'perhaps the horrible crime was committed in England. Could he have shot Owen?'

'He could, if he was crazy enough to think no one would

notice,' said Simon, answering the last question first. 'But, even if he did, why should he disappear? He could have no reason for thinking that we suspected him, because we didn't. And his agent couldn't suggest any possible link with Owen, though perhaps he'll be more informative now. The horrible crime in Italy is only a faint possibility; I shall have to check that with the Italian police. The idea of a temporary disappearance is even less likely, because he was due to fly back to Rome at 9.30 this morning. The fact that he's missed that plane does rather suggest that his disappearance may not be entirely voluntary. In other words, we have to ask ourselves whether anyone has a reason for wanting to keep him out of the way.'

'Do you think that Cassati could have *seen* the murderer— seen him actually fire the shot, I mean?'

'He wouldn't be likely to look behind. If he did see anyone using a pistol, it could only have been someone in the front row of the audience, or else the bass or the pianist.'

'You have no reason, have you,' suggested Mr Jones, 'to connect this affair necessarily with Owen's murder? They may be quite separate.'

'Of course,' Simon agreed. 'But it is a coincidence. I don't think I can completely ignore it. And anyway, he'll have to be found. It's possible that he may be a dangerous man and even more possible that he may be in some danger. I'm very much afraid that I shall have to go and help Bill look for him.'

He took a last nostalgic pull on his cigar and discarded it.

'Can I come too?' asked Delia. 'I think it's miserable for you, having to trail around on Christmas Day.'

'It certainly will be a trail, I warn you. It will be quite impossible to find out where anybody is and if we do catch up with someone at last, he'll be so angry at being disturbed that he won't tell us a thing. Also, it's against the rules. But,' he added hastily, 'if you'd really like to come, I'd love company.'

They went first to the hotel, which was anxious to be

helpful but had little to say. Signor Cassati had asked to be awakened at seven-thirty that morning and to have breakfast and his bill brought to his room at eight. The desk had been unable to get an answer at seven-thirty and so had instead aroused the gentleman's valet, who discovered that his master's bed had not been slept in. At eight-twenty a Daimler had called to take the tenor to the airport; its driver, who waited for an hour, claimed to have been given explicit instructions to call. At nine-fifteen the manager had been in touch with BEA and had discovered that Cassati had not reported for his seat on the aircraft, nor made any alternative arrangements.

Guido, the valet, appeared to speak every European language except English. Simon summoned all the French he could remember and managed to make his questions clear, if not gracefully expressed.

'You speak no English?'

'None at all.'

'Does Signor Cassati speak any?'

'Perfectly. He had many English friends during the war, you understand.'

Simon tightened his lips; he had heard that line before.

'When did you last see your employer?'

'A little before midnight last night at the Royal Opera House. You will understand that there were many friends who wished to congratulate him and to drink with him. It was not until late that he was able to change from his costume into his own clothes.'

'What was he wearing then? Tails?'

Guido had some difficulty in understanding the significance of the word which Simon had chosen to translate 'tails', but it was at last established that this was, in fact, his dress.

'And where is that suit now? In his room?'

'No. I have looked most carefully, and it is not there. In addition, there are no other clothes missing. I think he has not returned to the hotel since leaving the opera.'

'Where was he intending to go when he left you last night?'

'To the hotel, certainly. There was an invitation to a party, but I heard him tell the lady that he had to rise very early in the morning and that he could not come. I think it was true: Signor Cassati liked very much to sleep long in the night. Often, he did not rise until after lunch, and these early flights were not a pleasure to him.'

'Do you know whether he left the Opera House alone last night?'

'There was a lady with him as he left the room, but I think he was trying to get away from her. I do not think they would go anywhere together.'

'Can you describe the lady, by any chance?'

Guido clutched at the air with his hands in an effort to seize on some characteristic.

'She was a quite old lady, not like the other visitors,' he said at last. 'She was not gay, and I do not think Signor Cassati knew her before. She tried all the time in the party to speak to him, but always someone would interrupt, or, if no one came, then he would walk away himself and say "Yes, yes" as if he wished her to go.'

'But what did she look like?'

'She was not chic, even for an old lady. She wore a grey dress and a necklace of pearls, I think they were expensive, but so dull. Her hair was grey also, but had been dark, and it was too much over her face so that she looked heavy. She was not a woman one would notice.'

'Perhaps you could write down the names of some of the other people who visited the dressing-room—I suppose you announced them as they arrived. We may find someone who knows this lady.'

A little doubtfully, Guido wrote five or six names in the notebook he was offered, shrugging his shoulders over each.

'I do not know any more,' he said at last. 'But this one'—he pointed to a name—'is someone important in the Opera House; no doubt he would know them all.'

'How would Signor Cassati have intended to return to the hotel? By taxi?'

'No, there was a car. We have been in England six days, and all the time there has been a Daimler, which he hired—the same one all the time, you understand. Each time when he had finished, he would tell the driver when to come again. Last night it was to be at a quarter-past eleven. The car came, I know, because the door-keeper brought the message up to say that it waited.'

'And it came again this morning, so he must have seen the driver to give him fresh instructions.'

'It would seem so.'

'Were you at last Saturday's concert?'

'No, there was no need for me; he dressed at the hotel.'

'So you didn't see the death of the conductor. Did Signor Cassati mention it to you?'

'Yes, he was most distressed and agitated. He said many times the next day, "I did not think such assassinations were made in England."'

'Do you think that he knew anything about this death—that perhaps by chance he saw the murderer fire?'

'I am sure he did not. He told me in great detail and more than once of the happening, and each time it was with horror and shock, but nothing more.'

Simon consulted his notebook.

'Don't be afraid to answer my next question, Guido; it may be very important if we are to find your employer safely. Had he any reason that you know of for *needing* to disappear?'

The little Italian was up in arms at once.

'He was a great man,' he shouted in his own language and then repeated it in French. 'He had reasons only to be praised. I think he is held to ransom. You must find him quickly before he is harmed.'

'I'm sure we shall,' Simon soothed him. 'And in England people are not often stolen for money.' He shut his notebook, indicating that there were no further questions.

'What are you going to do now?' he asked. 'You'll wait on in England, I hope.'

'I think so, but not in this hotel. There is a question of expense. I must find a little place and then I will come here every day to make enquiries.'

Simon nodded.

'Leave your new address at the reception desk here then, so that we can get in touch with you as soon as we have some news. And here is my card. If by any chance you remember the name of the lady who left with Signor Cassati, please let me know at once.'

The valet bowed and left the room silently.

'Poor little man; he's upset about it, isn't he?' said Delia, getting up from the corner in which she had been sitting unobtrusively.

'Well, it's an unpleasant thing to be mixed up in, especially in a strange country where you don't speak the language. I'd better get on to the Daimler people—you can listen in on the extension if you like.'

A shift of duty on Christmas Day had no effect on the courteous good temper with which the call was answered. Simon introduced himself and asked for the name and address of the driver who had picked Cassati up at Covent Garden on the previous evening. There was a rustling of papers before the polite voice replied.

'It appears that our client was not called for at 11.15 after all.'

'Why not? He'd ordered the car then, hadn't he?'

'Yes, he did originally instruct the driver who took him to the Opera House to return at that time, but the instructions were cancelled later by telephone.'

'What did he say?'

'I understand that he had been invited to join His Excellency's party in honour of Her Royal Highness at the Embassy after the performance, and that one of the Embassy cars had been put at his disposal. It was not Signor Cassati himself who spoke, but his servant. We enquired whether he still required a car to take him to the airport this morning and were told to come as arranged.'

'When had that arrangement been made, then?'

'Oh, before Signor Cassati arrived in England. His agent gave us the times of his arrival and departure and instructed us to place a car at his disposal between those two times.'

'I'm very anxious to find out who it was who phoned to cancel the car last night. Did he speak good English?'

'Oh yes. He was an Englishman.'

'And did he definitely say that he was Signor Cassati's servant? It wasn't someone from the hotel or theatre?'

'I believe the word he used was valet.'

'Right. Well look, will you check up on where all your cars were just before midnight last night. If there's one you can't account for, let me know. There's no possibility, I suppose, that the driver made a mistake, or wasn't told, and turned up after all?'

'None at all. We're always very busy on Christmas Eve. As soon as the cancellation was received, the car and driver were assigned to another job.'

Simon thanked the polite young man and rang off.

'Will you do something for me?' he asked Delia. 'Go and find Guido—he'll probably be in Cassati's room—and ask him a question—about anything you like—what sort of shoes Cassati was wearing, for instance. Ask it in English and completely casually, as if you hadn't the faintest suspicion that he might not understand you.'

While she was gone, Simon busied himself on the telephone tracking down the Covent Garden stage doorkeeper. Delia returned within a few minutes.

'He just stared and then said, "I do not speak English; do you speak Italian, French, German?"' she reported. 'I'm sure it was genuine; he'd obviously learnt that much off by heart.'

'I thought so. Now we've got to find the man who phoned the Daimler Hire people—it's pretty clear that Cassati's been kidnapped for some reason. Well, the car you ordered is outside, madam. Would you care to step in and see where it takes you?'

'Where *is* it taking me?' Delia asked as they drove unbelievably fast through the empty streets of central London.

'To visit Mr. Perkins, who looks after the stage door at Covent Garden and who also, by the best of luck, is a retired policeman and willing to interrupt even his daughter's Christmas party in such a good cause as that of crime.'

He missed a road island by inches and decided belatedly that it was time he switched his lights on.

It took a certain amount of search and enquiry to find Palladian Place in Islington. When at last they arrived outside the narrow terrace house they found to their surprise that it was completely dark and silent. Through a crack between two curtains they could see the flickering of a coal fire, but apart from that the house seemed deserted.

'He promised he'd be in,' Simon said in a worried voice, fishing in his notebook to check the address. Tentatively he rang the bell.

There was a second's silence; no more. Then Delia's heart jumped at the sound of a piercing, prolonged scream. She clutched Simon's arm nervously, but already his mouth was turning up into a smile. For all over the house lights were being switched on; there was an incredible noise of shouting and laughter and, as Mr. Perkins opened the door for them, the two visitors saw apparently hundreds of youngsters tumbling down the narrow stairs and into the room where the fire burned.

'Come in, Superintendent,' he said cheerfully. 'I hope you don't mind if I take you into the kitchen. It's a mess, but it's out of bounds. They're playing Murder in all the rest of the house, so this is the only place where we can be safe from attack.'

He closed the door and led the way. The kitchen certainly was not at its tidiest, piled high with the debris of a party tea. Mr. Perkins cleared a dish of trifle and a crumpled pile of paper hats off a rocking-chair for Delia and waved a hospitable hand over the table.

'I don't know if you've had your tea,' he invited, 'but we'd be glad if you could give us a hand with any of this. Otherwise, we shall be having jelly for breakfast for a week.'

Delia shook her head smilingly, but Simon had already forgotten his enormous lunch and was admiring the ruins on the table, wondering in astonishment how much there must have been before the noisy gang of youngsters had helped themselves.

'Well,' he said frankly. 'That cake looks very good.'

He had hardly spoken before a thick wedge was in his hand, making the whole of the subsequent conversation a struggle between temptation and good manners.

'I've come about last night,' he said, realising just in time that the robin in his mouth was not intended to be swallowed. 'We've lost Cassati—the Italian tenor—and I'm hoping you may be able to give us a lead. You know what he looks like, I suppose.'

'He was pointed out to me in the afternoon; he came in for rehearsal. Not much impressed, I wasn't, but Mother heard him on the wireless and said he sang a treat.'

'We want to know what happened when he left. Do you remember the time, any companions, what sort of car he used?'

'Yes, I can tell you all that. The car was a Daimler, same as he came in. It turned up about eleven and I sent a message up, but it was nearer twelve before they got away. Bit of a party going on upstairs, I dare say. There was quite a crowd waiting for them all to come out—they saw the Royals off at the front and then came round to my door. Freezing cold it was, too, but you'd be surprised how many of them were still there at half-past eleven. After that they got a bit browned off and started drifting away. As for companions, he came downstairs with a lady, an elderly lady. Don't know who she was. But as soon as he saw his car, he jumped for it and left her on the pavement, quite rude like. Left her in the middle of a sentence, I wouldn't be surprised. She looked a bit put out. She asked me for a taxi, but I told her to go round to the front, so I didn't see what happened to her.'

'And meanwhile the Daimler had moved off?'

'That's right. Only one way it could go in that street, of course. The driver seemed to know where to go; I didn't see the gentleman say anything to him.'

'I suppose you didn't notice anything particular about the Daimler—it wasn't in fact the same one that came before the performance.'

'Wasn't it now? Well, I'm afraid one Daimler's the same as another to me, except for the number, and I'd no reason to look at that. Wait a minute, though. I had my daughter in with me last night, being holidays. She likes to look at the dresses, you know. She collects car numbers, and I remember her squealing that she'd seen a 365. But, of course, that might have been any of the cars. Hold on a minute, will you.'

He opened the kitchen door and shouted into the house in general.

'Nellie! Come down into the kitchen a minute, will you. I won't keep you a sec.'

There was a sound of adolescent giggling.

'I can't, Dad. I'm dead.'

'Well, come and be dead down here, then, and hurry.'

Nellie hurried, giving a good imitation of the charge of the Heavy Brigade. The sight of the kitchen table, however, destroyed any feeling of sulkiness she might have felt, and she sucked at chocolate fingers while she stared at the two strangers.

'Nellie,' said Mr. Perkins. 'You know that 365 you got last night. Happen to remember what sort of a car it was?'

'Rolls,' said Nellie briefly.

'Are you quite sure?' persisted her father. 'Mind, it's important now.'

''Course I'm sure,' Nellie replied scornfully. 'You can't make mistakes with Rollses.'

'I suppose you didn't happen to notice the number of the Daimler that was parked outside between about eleven and twelve.'

'Old Fatty's? Yes, I did, because it was a 368. I kept wondering whether the other two in between might come along before it went so that I could count it.'

'That's wonderful,' said Simon, digging for his notebook. 'What about the letters? Do you remember them?'

''Fraid not. I only need the letters when I put them in the book. I don't notice them otherwise.'

'Never mind. That's helped enormously,' congratulated Simon. 'Thank you very much. Have another chocolate biscuit.'

'She'll be sick,' said her father, but he watched indulgently as she took three and rushed from the kitchen with a sudden warlike yell. 'Think you'll get it just on the numbers?'

'Well, there aren't so many Daimlers, are there? I think it will be very useful. Tell me, did you get a glimpse of the driver of the car that last time?'

'Not to speak of, I'm afraid. He came and told me he was there, so to speak, but I didn't look at him properly. He was wearing a dark peaked cap and raincoat like they always do—in fact, I took it for granted he was the same chappie that I'd seen driving before. Never gave it a thought, to tell you the truth.'

'Why should you?' Simon said sadly. 'Well, I'm sorry to have interrupted your Christmas. We'll leave you to it now.'

'Glad of a minute's peace,' Mr. Perkins said frankly, leading the way to the door. 'Now into the fray once more for both of us. Merry Christmas.'

It was cold outside. Delia hugged herself to stop her sudden shivering and Simon took the hint and hugged her as well. He started the car with some difficulty and dawdled along until he saw a telephone booth. Leaving Delia with an apology, he rang the Missing Persons Bureau.

'That you, Bill? Simon here. Found Cassati yet?'

There was a groan from the other end and Simon outlined his conversations of the afternoon. 'So work on the assumption that the disappearance is involuntary and find the Daimler. I should get a warning out to all road patrols, though it's probably too late to catch it, and check with stolen cars, self-drive hire agencies and all the Daimler agents. You're off tomorrow, I suppose. Well, leave a report on my desk. It looks as though I shall have to come in.'

This conclusion he repeated gloomily to Delia as he turned the car's nose towards her home.

'Tomorrow will be a hell of dullness,' he moaned. 'I shall spend all day worrying and waiting for something to happen, and nothing will happen at all.'

In that forecast, as it turned out, he was quite correct. Neither on Saturday nor on Sunday did he make any progress. But on Monday morning, doors began to open.

CHAPTER THIRTEEN

Dear Sir (the letter read),

I shall sign this letter Mary Smith, but it is not my real name, for reasons which you will appreciate in a moment. I am writing in connection with the death of Owen Burr, the conductor, in the RFH on Saturday, and I am writing because I do not want anyone to be accused of the murder unjustly. I shot him, with his own pistol which I took from his room a month ago. I am expecting a baby in May and Owen was its father. I only let him because he said he would marry me, and he was the first. And then he told me that he was going to be a great musician and not a trollop's husband and I was very angry because he would not marry me.

He told me on Saturday, and I went with the pistol, but I did not mean to shoot him but only to frighten him by threatening to shoot myself. But he would not see me in the interval, and, while I was listening, the music gave me a headache, and I was very unhappy, and I shot him. Now I am sorry, and I will always be sorry, but it is too late to do anything except see that no one else gets the blame instead of me. I suppose they wouldn't be able to hang me now, but I do not want to go to prison either, and that is why I have borrowed someone else's typewriter and shall post this where I do not live, but it is true all the same.

Yours truly,
Mary Smith.

Simon read the letter through again as he perched on the corner of his desk, faintly bad-tempered at Monday's return to work after what had proved to be hardly a holiday at all. Then he put it down and examined the envelope closely. It was a cheap white one, not matching the shiny blue paper inside, and the post-mark was thick and indistinct. Simon eventually decided that it was SW3, but the date surprised him, and he rang for Flint.

'What do you make that date?' he asked.

The sergeant peered and finally pronounced for December 23rd, 7.30 am.

'Yes, that's what I thought. And it's the twenty-eighth today. Where's it been all this time? That's Wednesday morning—probably posted on Tuesday night—and it's only just reached my desk. I was in on Saturday and it certainly wasn't here then. Either someone's been inefficient or else the postmark's been faked.'

'Well, sir, it was Christmas, you know. The Post Office said on the wireless that it was a heavy year for mail. Perhaps it was posted too late to be delivered before Christmas Day, and after that I think they slack up a bit.'

Simon snorted.

'All these people who get holidays at Christmas! I'd forgotten about them. Well look, Sergeant, get me a copy of this letter and take it down to be tested for finger-prints—it'll have mine, of course, but they've got them in the files. Tell them to photograph it; I want the letter back as soon as possible.'

Before he had time, however, to ponder further on the

appearance of Mary Smith in the case, the house telephone rang.

'Bill here. That Daimler of yours has been reported found.'

'Found! Don't you mean stolen?'

'Nope. Found by an insurance firm in Holborn—in their director's garage. There's a row of garages in a mews behind the buildings and apparently this firm rents one of them. The managing director went off on Thursday evening, leaving the garage empty and the door pulled across but not bolted—he said the lock is an awkward one and he doesn't bother with it when the garage is empty. Anyway, when he arrived this morning, there was this Daimler, PLB 368, sitting there as if it had lived there all its life.'

'Anything interesting about it?'

'The mileage is no good because we don't know when it went out. There are some splashes of mud on the sides, but they might have been there before. Anyway, I thought you'd like to know. It shouldn't be long before we're able to trace the owner now.'

'Thanks.'

Simon returned to Mary Smith. In the absence of any proof that Cassati's disappearance was linked with Owen's death, he felt he must concentrate on the latter, leaving the routine work to Bill. But he was disturbed almost immediately by a second peal on the telephone.

'I say, it's me again. We've had the "reported stolen" now—from the garage next to the one where it was found. It belongs to a firm of art dealers; they use a Daimler for making a good impression when they want to buy up a stately home. It was left locked up, but the lock has been picked. It looks as if the thief made a careless mistake, putting it back in the wrong place. Easy thing to do, though; they're not numbered. Anyway, the car could have been taken any time after four on Thursday, which is when they all knocked off; they haven't been near the place since and only discovered the loss half an hour ago. But the interesting thing is this: the last time it was used was for a private joyride by the general manager and, being a scrupulous sort of chap, he made a note of the mileage figures—and he cleaned it when he got back. So I am now in a position to state that our kidnapper drove a little under forty miles in his wicked weekend, taking in at least one dirty puddle *en route*.'

'Keep at it,' said Simon. 'There can't be many mud puddles within a radius of twenty miles of Holborn. Now leave me to my own little headaches.'

He returned yet again to the problem of Mary Smith, reading and re-reading the copy which Flint had brought into him and trying to decide why it should ring so false. He was used to receiving confessions of murder from people who had probably never killed anything much larger than a wasp, but they bore on almost all occasions the writer's correct name and address to ensure that they would receive full notoriety. That fact did not prove that this letter had any stronger basis of truth, of course, and with each reading Simon became more undecided. He rejected it on its face value, but there was another possibility—that the letter was indeed written by the murderer, but carefully giving an invented character and motive for the murder in order to disguise the real one. And unless John Southerley was a nervous type, there was only one man who had reason to be seriously alarmed about the suspicions of the police—and that man had been in Italy when the letter was postmarked. If he had posted it himself, he could not possibly have reached Chelsea after his conversation with Simon at the airport and returned in time to catch his plane.

Simon pulled the telephone towards him and dialled Delia's office number. There was no reply, and he sighed with envy of anyone whose employers were kind enough to add an extra day to the Christmas holiday, and whose work would wait for it. He found her at home, however, and she agreed to meet him for lunch 'on condition you take two hours, to make it worth the journey'. He promised, having every intention of making them a profitable two hours from the point of view of his work. In the meantime, he had a visit to pay.

As soon as he opened the door of Owen's flat, he heard the sound of papers rustling. Kicking himself mentally for having taken the guard off the building too soon, he tiptoed into the living-room. Shirley Marsden was there, kneeling on the floor with a drawer from Owen's desk in front of her. Simon coughed gently and Shirley jumped up with a little scream.

'Oh!' she gasped. 'You frightened me. I didn't know anyone else had a key to the flat.'

'I didn't know anyone else had a key to this desk, either.'

'Oh yes, I've had that for a couple of years. Some of the papers in it were mine, you see. Sometimes we used to work on them together, but often I wanted to get on by myself; Owen had another key cut specially so that I wouldn't have to wait if he were out.'

'I see. Just hold on a minute while I go back and shut the front door, will you—I thought you were a burglar.'

He walked heavily from the room but in the corridor outside, while he could still see the desk, he went no further, although his feet continued their heavy tread—on the spot. He saw what he had half expected—a pair of hands feverishly searching through the pigeon-holes at the top of the desk. A bundle of papers was extracted; Simon risked leaning back-wards until he could see Shirley. She had risen and was stuffing the papers into her handbag; they were too bulky, so she pushed them instead into the pockets of her overcoat, which lay loosely across a chair.

Simon continued more genuinely on his way to the front door. When he returned, Shirley was kneeling on the floor as he had left her, although perhaps a little pinker in the face.

'Now then, perhaps you'd tell me about these papers, would you, Miss Marsden?'

She was eager to do so; her embarrassment at being found in what she herself obviously regarded as suspicious circumstances sent the words tumbling out of her mouth.

'We were writing a book together, Owen and I, you see. It was going to be called *The Lyrical Element in Modern Music.* It was really a series of essays about some modern composers. Owen chose the composers and did the actual writing of the essays. The idea was his in the first place, and all the theories. I did the research for him—you know, collected any articles or reviews on the same theme. But my chief job was to find musical quotations to illustrate his theories. He'd just make a note, for instance, "Try Lennox Berkeley's Piano Concerto", and I'd have to read through the full score till I found the bit he wanted, and then copy it out.'

'It sounds a very specialised job,' said Simon, honestly impressed.

'It's only a matter of education, really. I was taught to read scores when I was quite young, and now I don't find it much more difficult than a child does to pick out a tune on one finger. Anyway, I've been thinking about this all week since Owen died, and yesterday I decided that I ought to finish the book for him. I thought it would be nice to have it published under his name as a sort of memorial. He'd finished half of it properly; the rest is all in note form, but of course we've discussed it together a lot, so it wouldn't be too difficult. I could finish it in three months, I think.'

'You don't have a job, then?'

'No. My parents let me have enough to live on and it seems silly to tie oneself down when there are always interesting things turning up. Is it all right for me to take these papers away? I feel they're as much mine as his. I've nearly finished sorting them.'

'I'm afraid you can't just disappear with them. Suppose you put everything you want to take in one pile and let me look through it. I'll let you know when I've checked that there's nothing helpful there. Then you'll have to clear it with his executors.'

She nodded and continued to sort through the drawer in front of her. It was neatly arranged, and she clearly knew what she was looking for. Some files were rejected at once; others were placed with equal decision on her own pile. At last she sat back on her ankles.

'That's all I need to take. I can leave you the key of the desk now.'

Simon looked at her in silence for a moment longer.

'You're going to put those letters in your coat pocket back in the desk then, are you?'

He saw the blood creep up her neck, then sink to leave her face unnaturally pale. She did not speak to deny what she had taken but waited, staring at him.

'May I look?' He pulled the bundle from her pocket.

'They're private,' she snapped before he had time to look at any of the letters he held. 'I wrote them all. I have a right to take them back.'

'Well, we won't go into that now. Why should you want them back?'

Shirley blushed again, but this time with modesty rather than guilt.

'They're love letters. I don't particularly want to have strangers reading them.'

'I'm sorry, Miss Marsden. I can't let anything out of this flat until I've inspected it.'

He had in fact glanced briefly at the letters and presumed them to be unhelpful when he made his first inspection of the flat and its contents; only Shirley's anxiety now renewed his interest in them. It was possible that she was in fact modest, but the queenly confidence of her good looks made this seem unlikely to someone who did not know her well. In any case, having made his decision he was not prepared to argue about it; he changed the subject quickly.

'I wonder if you'd tell me, Miss Marsden, where you last saw this pistol?'

He produced it from his pocket, the pistol which had killed Owen, and held it before her. She stared at it without any sign of recognition.

'I've never seen it before at all.'

'Yet I believe it belonged to Mr. Burr. Wouldn't you have noticed it around the flat?'

'Not necessarily. I never searched the flat or anything like that. If he kept it hidden, there would be no reason for me to know about it. But are you sure it was his? It's most unlike him, you know. He had terrifically strong arms and hands and he always boasted that he could get the better of anyone who tried to attack him. I can't think why he should want to buy a gun.'

Simon, agreeing privately, pressed on to the next question. He expected a strong reaction and he was by no means disappointed.

'To change the subject, Miss Marsden, did you know that Mr. Burr was about to become a father?'

'That's not true!' Shirley sprang to her feet, her eyes blazing. 'You've just made it up. It can't possibly be true.'

'Why not, Miss Marsden? Because he was in love with you?'

'It's nothing to do with that. He wasn't that sort of man.'

'I'm afraid a good many men are that sort of man, on one or two occasions in their lives at least. Why should your man be an exception?'

'Because—because he was dedicated. Don't you understand what I mean? Do you think I wouldn't have been his mistress if he really wanted me, but he didn't—or at least, he did, but he wouldn't. That was why he wouldn't marry me, as well, although he wanted to, and he was always just going to arrange it. He had a sort of theory that he would lose something—energy, or virtue, or whatever you like to call it—that must on no account be lost but must be put into his music instead. I'm afraid I'm explaining very badly, but I'm quite sure he was sincere. I'm certain you've made a mistake.'

Simon saw how deeply he had hurt her and was ashamed of himself.

'Yes, I'm sure I have, Miss Marsden. In fact, I must apologise for putting it to you so much as if it were certain. I was only quoting a letter I have received, which I am quite unable to check. I've no doubt it was written by some sensationalist who never met Mr. Burr in her life.'

He watched her emotions sinking once more under control.

'I suppose you knew about Evan Tredegar being his father, did you?'

'Yes. Owen told me about a week before he died. I think he had only just found out.'

'What was his reaction to the discovery?'

'Well, he'd had a few days to think about it when he told me, but he was still pretty excited. He'd always guessed that his father must be a rich man, because of the way money was pumped into his bank account ever since he was a schoolboy. And he'd even wondered about the Old Man—giving him the job with the Metro and being helpful in other ways. When he was sure of the truth, I think he hoped to persuade the Old Man to help him more openly.'

'What were his feelings towards Mr. Tredegar, do you know?'

'Until he found out about this business, he had a lot of respect for him. Afterwards, I think he was a little resentful that he hadn't been given a proper home after his mother died. He hadn't really had time to settle down into the relationship, though. I say, I'm afraid I must go now. I've promised to meet John Southerley for lunch.'

'He's a friend of yours, is he?' Simon enquired.

'Well, I've known him for a couple of years, of course. He's not a particular friend. But he's been kind to me this last week. Everyone else has been leaving me severely alone, as if I wouldn't be able to bear any company. But he realised I'd be lonely and—well, he's been making me talk. I'm very grateful to him.'

'I'm sure you are. Well then, I mustn't keep you. Will you leave the keys of the desk and the flat with me, please?'

She handed them over, looked mournfully round the owner-less room and left. Simon remained; for ten minutes he stood without moving as he thought, then, until it was time for him to meet Delia, he began to re-read the papers which Shirley had set aside. The musical efficiency of her notes and the passionate language of her letters impressed him equally: they revealed the two sides of Owen's character as well as of Shirley's. And there was one side which Simon found himself increasingly forced to admire; admiration came more easily, he suspected, now that death had removed the other, more infuriating, characteristics. Who else could it be, he wondered, who might also have hated the man too deeply to allow the musician to survive?

CHAPTER FOURTEEN

Simon ordered coffee and passed Mary Smith's letter across the table.

'What do you make of this?' he asked.

Delia read it with a frown.

'It's a queer sort of letter, isn't it? Is it true?'

'You know as much about that as I do. What would you say?'

She considered it again before answering.

'I don't think it is. I think Owen was too fastidious to have anything to do with anyone he would describe as a trollop—it was a word he did use, as a matter of fact. I imagine he'd got Shirley or could have her if he wanted to. And there's something phoney about the letter—as if it were by someone who normally writes good English but is deliberately trying to sound common and only succeeding in patches.' She read it through again. 'There's one other slightly odd thing as well. Most people talk about the Festival Hall; the only people who would say RFH would be those who are in the habit of mentioning it in correspondence.'

'Such as.'

'Well, such as Shirley, or Mrs Bainsbury, or the Old Man.'

'Or John Southerley?'

'Perhaps. Not so likely.'

'That's very interesting. I was wondering about Shirley myself. I've just been talking to her and it seemed to me that she had good reason to be jealous of music; she might have been angry because she *wasn't* expecting a baby.'

'Shirley would never be jealous of music,' Delia said confidently. 'And I'm sure she really was in love with Owen. She wouldn't break her own heart by killing him. Surely the Old Man is the most likely of those three. After all, I presume there's a good chance, isn't there, that this letter was written either by the murderer or by someone who knew he was suspected of murder and wanted to get you on to a different track?'

'I don't think it could have been posted by the Old Man. I've checked at the airport and none of the staff admits to having taken it for him. And there wasn't anyone else who need have felt himself dangerously under suspicion.'

'Oh.' Delia was silent for a moment, while Simon waited for her to produce one of her bright ideas. It came as he had hoped.

'Look, suppose the murderer was a rather squeamish, scrupulous sort of murderer. He found out that the Old Man was going to get the blame and so he felt he must divert you but daren't do it, of course, with the truth. In other words, perhaps the spirit of the letter is genuine, although none of the facts are.'

'That theory would appear to leave us with Mrs Bainsbury as the murderer. You'd be prepared to accept that, would you?'

'No, I wouldn't really. After all, I was standing next to her. I can't believe that a pistol could be fired so near to me without my knowing about it.'

'There was a lot of noise going on at the time, you know.'

'Yes, but even so, murder isn't a thing one does casually, I imagine. As soon as our actual singing part was over that evening, we all relaxed, even while the orchestra was still playing. If the person next to me had still been tense instead of relaxing, I'm sure I should have been aware of it. One tends to be sensitive at a time like that. But of course, Mary Smith may not be anything to do with the Metro; she certainly doesn't have to be one of those three.'

'How depressingly right you are. All the same, you haven't a specimen of Mrs Bainsbury's typewriting anywhere, have you?'

'I expect I've got an old agenda at home somewhere. I usually make notes on them, so I keep them for a bit. I'll put it in the post this afternoon if you like.'

'Do. Because although it doesn't *have* to be anyone we know about already, who but the people who heard you phone last Tuesday would know that the Old Man—or anyone else—was under suspicion?'

'Is he still, by the way?'

Simon shrugged his shoulders.

'I'm just as I was. I do know that he wasn't directly connected with Cassati's disappearance, though, because I've had a man on his tail ever since he returned to England. That's another queer thing—Cassati. Whose idea was it that you should have him?'

'Shirley's, I think. Mrs Bainsbury would tell you for certain from the Minutes. Shirley was the only one who knew in advance that he was coming to England.'

'How did she find out that, do you think?'

'One of the Covent Garden tenors is a friend of her family. I expect he told them. It wouldn't be a secret.'

'I suppose not. Well, I must go and pay a call on your treasurer. I've had an accountant working on his books and checking them with the bank's figures and he says that all is not completely well with them.'

'I hope you have an appointment, then. He's terribly fussy about being disturbed at work.'

Simon did have an appointment. This did not save him from a ten-minute wait in a secretary's office, but he passed the time profitably in persuading her to give him a sample of typewriting done on her machine. When he was at last admitted to the insurance agent's room, he noticed at once the extreme nervousness of Robert Stanley, who lost no time in making clear his resentment of this intrusion.

'I hope you will be able to dispose of your business quickly, Superintendent. I do not normally approve of devoting my office hours to the affairs of the Metro. However, I presume that you are still investigating Owen's death.'

'Indirectly, yes. I'm also trying to find out something more about Cassati. I've been looking through your accounts and I see that his fee is down as fifty guineas, paid. There isn't any possibility of a mistake there, by any chance?'

'No. What sort of a mistake?'

'Well, Cassati's agent says he has received a hundred guineas —the usual fee, apparently. It's only a minor point, but surprising, so I thought I'd check it.'

'No one has ever mentioned the figure of a hundred to me: if that had been his fee, we should have been unable to book him. I should hardly be likely to make a mistake of that sort in my entry.'

Simon smiled blandly.

'Of course not. Any mistakes you make are more likely to be on the other side, aren't they, Mr Stanley?'

The other man's face first whitened and then flushed.

'I'm afraid I don't know what you are talking about. You sound as if your intention is to be insulting.'

'Oh no, Mr Stanley. But you do seem to have had trouble once or twice with the Metro's accounts, don't you—surprising, really, for a man in your position who must be used to dealing with figures. There was that business eight years ago, for example. It was getting very complicated, wasn't it, until you managed to pay £800 into the Metro's account. Yet at that time your own account had been overdrawn consistently for almost a year. Where did the money come from, Mr Stanley?' He added, as he saw the other's eyes desperately searching: 'You might as well tell me the truth, you know. It saves so much misunderstanding in the end.'

The answer came grudgingly, but Simon accepted it as true.

'It came from Evan Tredegar.'

'Why should he go to that expense?'

'He was a friend of mine, he was a friend of the choir's, and he was rich.'

'He must have been a very good friend of yours. Was the money a gift or a loan?'

'A gift. I was in a difficult situation just then. There would have been no hope of my repaying a loan.'

'And Owen knew about it?'

'It was he who brought it all up. I'd hoped that I should be able to straighten things up before the audit, but then Owen arrived on the scene and wanted the books before he started, to see how things stood. I didn't have time to do anything about them and he soon noticed what was wrong and told Evan.'

'Tell me, Mr Stanley, did he ever try to blackmail you?'

'Not that time. Evan wouldn't have let him.'

'Not that time! But perhaps the next time—that was two years ago, wasn't it? I'm surprised that Mr Tredegar hadn't suggested that you should resign before that.'

'He did, but I was ashamed and wanted to make amends by doing the job properly. And the second time wasn't so serious. I'd only borrowed a little money to pay for a summer holiday. I paid it back within two months.'

'But in that two months Owen discovered it?'

'Yes.'

'What did he do? Use threats to get money out of you?'

'Oh no.' Stanley looked genuinely shocked. 'No, he didn't blackmail me in any criminal sense—he never said anything openly. He just let me know that he knew, and, then whenever he wanted something, he would mention it indirectly, as if he were teasing me, to make sure that I didn't stop him.'

'What sort of thing do you mean that he wanted?'

'Well, it usually happened at Metro committee meetings—for example, if he wanted to book a particular soloist for a concert and he could see that I was just going to say that we couldn't afford it.'

Simon stared in surprise.

'Do you mean to say that he only used this discovery of his to get what he wanted musically—never for his own advantage?'

'That is correct. If he had asked for money, of course I should have had to come out with the whole business. But the things he wanted—two extra trumpets or a top-rank soprano or whatever it was—always seemed so reasonable that I never thought it worthwhile to make a fuss.'

Simon looked squarely across the table.

'Would you be prepared, Mr Stanley, to repeat everything that you have told me here on oath, as being nothing but the truth?'

'I would.'

Still staring, Simon felt inclined to believe him. The treasurer was clearly much more at ease now that he had relieved his mind of its fretting anxiety. Moreover, unlikely though the story might sound at first hearing, it fitted in with the picture of Owen on which everyone seemed to agree—that of the monomaniac, the fanatical musician. He wondered whether there was anything more to be said and as he sat in silence his fingers played with a leaflet arranged on the edge of the table in a position where it was obviously meant to attract the attention of visitors. It showed pictorially the advantages to be gained (by one's widow) of insuring one's life. Fleetingly, as he stood up to go, Simon wondered whether Delia would appreciate such a gesture if...Then his mind gave a jerk and his wandering eyes steadied.

'I suppose that as a friend of Mr Tredegar's who deals in insurance, you'd be given any business of that sort to do for him?'

Robert Stanley stood up also, smiling in his relief that the interview was ending.

'I don't think that sort of thing has ever attracted him. He has no dependants, and quite enough money to last his own lifetime.'

'I was thinking actually of the policy he took out on Owen Burr's life. You did that for him, did you?'

A shutter came down. Stanley stopped dead with his hand on the door. Then he smiled with polite vagueness.

'On Owen's life? That does not sound very likely. I think you must have made a mistake there, Superintendent.'

'I will ask you a direct question. Were you aware that such a policy existed?'

'It seems to me most unlikely. In a case like that, where there is no relationship, a reason would have to be given for such an action.'

'That is exactly why it occurred to me that a friend in the insurance world might be useful, Mr Stanley. I'm sorry you don't feel able to be frank. Mr Tredegar told me about the existence of the policy himself, so I am sure he will be quite ready to give me further details.'

He could see as he watched that his guess had been correct. He was hardly sure why he had bothered to make it until he heard himself make one parting, unanswered remark.

'Shielding Mr Tredegar is a very dangerous hobby, Mr Stanley—and not least, of course, for Mr Tredegar.'

As he hurried down the stairs and along the street, he was pleased with his exit line but not sure, on reflection, that it had been of any constructive value. It was difficult to credit Robert Stanley with the imagination to become Mary Smith. Simon hailed a bus and found himself after a snail's progress down Oxford Street outside the office of Jack Higgins, musical agent.

Mr Higgins had been educated past his name. Opulence gleamed from the polish of his bald head to that of his hand-made shoes. He spoke smoothly, if over-ornately, and his welcome to Simon left nothing to be desired.

'Come in, Superintendent. What will you have to drink? I know I needn't ask whether you've found my client yet. I've had one of your pals in an hour ago and he knows as much about it as I do.'

'Does that distress you, Mr Higgins?'

The agent threw two fleshy hands outwards.

'I met Cassati for the first time ten days ago. I'm only acting as a sub-agent for his Rome manager. This is the first time he's visited England professionally.'

'That's surprising, since I understand he speaks English perfectly. How did he pick it up?'

'I said professionally. He was at school here for five years as a boy. Hated every minute of it, he told me. His father was a rich silver merchant, but *he* never got further here than being called a dirty little Italian. Mind you, he wanted to come over in 1948 for a tour but I advised against it. Too soon after the war, I told him, and he was mixed up in it. Might have caused feeling.'

'Good heavens,' said Simon. 'You're not going to tell me that with a figure like that Cassati was in the Army!'

'Funny, isn't it. To look at him you'd think he'd devote all his energy to finding some nice soft corner. Good excuse, a voice like that, too. But not a bit of it. He was one of the real Fascists —a personal pal of some of the high-ups. He volunteered as soon as the war started for Italy—wouldn't be kept out. Mind you, I don't think he ever did any actual fighting. But for a couple of years he was on the staff of a POW camp in North Italy—run by Germans, with a lot of British prisoners there. And he made some pretty hot speeches too, especially just before the war began. People don't remember, though. No complaints at all this year, not even letters, and you'd be surprised at what I get with some of these foreign singers. You have to prove that they spent the war in Belsen before some people will be satisfied. However, I suppose you've got something to ask me, haven't just come for the pleasure of my company.'

'It's a small point, Mr Higgins, but it's been puzzling me. When I came in last week your young lady told me that the Metro had paid a hundred guineas for that concert, but they seem to think they only paid fifty. Can you straighten it out?'

Mr. Higgins swung in his chair towards a green steel cabinet and pulled out a drawer. From the file he extracted he chose a bundle of letters pinned together and studied them.

'Quite right,' he said. 'It was a bit queer. I thought they wouldn't have him, and then they booked him after all, but Mrs Bainsbury—that's their secretary—asked me to send two bills to her, each for fifty guineas and each made out as if it were the only one. I thought it was a bit odd, but the Metro are good customers of mine, so I did it and the whole lot was paid all right. One cheque was signed by Stanley and Bainsbury as usual and the other by J. Sheraton-Smith. Who *he* is you'd have to find out from Mrs Bainsbury.'

'May I do that now, on your telephone?'

'Certainly, Superintendent, certainly.'

He pushed the telephone across his desk and tactfully engrossed himself in a sheaf of press-cuttings while Simon elicited from a doubtful Mrs Bainsbury the address of Mrs Sheraton-Smith.

To this address, in a massive Kensington Crescent, Simon made his way at once and was shown by a young maid into a drawing-room furnished almost entirely, it seemed, with unsteady occasional tables and silver-framed photographs. In the middle of this gallery Mrs Sheraton-Smith was pouring herself tea from a silver teapot. She received the announcement of Simon's name and business with a smoothly vague politeness that had doubtless been perfected in many decades of At Homes. Simon came quickly to the point of his visit.

'Would you mind telling me what is your special interest in Signor Cassati, Mrs Sheraton-Smith?'

'Could you speak a little louder, Superintendent?'

Simon repeated his enquiry.

'I understand that he is a very fine tenor. Will you help yourself to sugar?'

'Thank you. But there must have been some more cogent reason that would persuade you to contribute such a large sum in order to bring him to England. You must have wanted him to come very badly.'

'It was not too large a sum to me. And of course he was coming to England anyway; I was not interested in arranging that. My only wish was to help the Metro to make the Mass a really great occasion. And so they would have done, had it not been for poor Owen's death. But do you know, I understand that now they are being flooded with applications to join the choir, and I very much fear it is because of the newspaper reports of the murder. It is pathetic, is it not, that people should be so anxious to associate themselves with a sensation?'

'Have you ever given money to the Metro before, Mrs Sheraton-Smith?'

'Yes, indeed I have. It is very difficult for a choir of this sort, which feels some sense of duty to living composers, to survive in the musical world of today. Everything is so expensive; although the choir itself is amateur—no choir of that size could hope to be anything else—yet the orchestra, the soloists, the management of the hall, the printers, all expect very large sums of money and few concert-goers seem prepared to pay the economic price for their seats—or indeed, in the case of the more modern composers, to pay any price at all. Bach and

Handel are always financially sound, of course, but I am glad to say that Mr Tredegar has never allowed the choir to limit its repertory merely to the safe works. So on many occasions there have been considerable financial losses. I am by no means the only person to have come to the rescue at such a time, and it has never occurred to me before that any reason was necessary apart from the facts of the case.'

Simon drank his tea slowly; he was not quite satisfied. The explanation seemed simple and reasonable enough to be true, and yet the speaker did not quite carry conviction. She was too consciously trying to keep the tea-party a normal social occasion at which no inconvenient remarks would be passed. Perhaps it was only his imagination. He tried to startle her by an abrupt change of subject.

'Do you possess a typewriter, Mrs Sheraton-Smith?'

'Yes, I possess one, but I do not use it. My late husband purchased it two years before he died. I am not quite certain where it is now, but doubtless my maid will know.'

She stretched a ringed hand towards the bell, but Simon interrupted before she could reach it.

'Please don't trouble her now. If you will allow me, I will ask her to let me have a look at it when she shows me out. I've just one other question. Did you meet Signor Cassati personally during his visit to England?'

'I was present at a party in his dressing-room on Christmas Eve. It was very much as all parties of that sort are and I went without invitation. I am sure that if you were to ask him, he would have no recollection of meeting me.'

'Good heavens!' exclaimed Simon, looking at his hostess as if for the first time. 'Was it you who was with him when he left the theatre?'

'As long as my answer does not imply that I did more than reach the stage door at the same moment,' said Mrs Sheraton-Smith, 'then I can say that that is so.'

CHAPTER FIFTEEN

'Mrs. Sheraton-Smith, do you never read the newspapers?'

Simon spoke indignantly, his relief at having discovered the mysterious companion overshadowed by the knowledge of how nearly he had missed the discovery.

'Never,' Mrs. Sheraton-Smith said decisively. She moved the tea-table slightly away from her chair as an indication that the visit could now politely be brought to an end. 'There is never anything in them of the slightest interest. Why should you suddenly ask that?'

'If you had read even a single newspaper you would have known how very anxious I was to talk to you, if only I could find out who you were.'

'Well, now you are talking to me, Superintendent, so all is well. Why did you want to find me?'

'I'd like to know, for one thing, what you were talking about just before you left the theatre.'

'I'm afraid I can't tell you, Superintendent. But if you were so anxious to know, surely you could have asked Signor Cassati himself that when you could not find me—or has he returned to

Italy by now? I suppose he has.'

'I have no idea where he is, Mrs. Sheraton-Smith. He has not been seen since he left you to step into his car.'

'Oh, I see. Perhaps he has gone into a monastery.'

Mrs. Sheraton-Smith appeared to think that this would be the most natural solution of the mystery. Simon stared at her in slight exasperation.

'Have you any reason to suppose that he contemplated such a step?'

'No, none at all. But he is a Roman Catholic, isn't he?'

Simon sighed gently.

'Did he discuss his future plans with you that evening at all? Did he say where he was going when he left the theatre?'

'He said he was going home to bed. He repeated it twice, I believe. He seemed very insistent on how tired he was.'

'Did you by any chance hear what directions he gave to the driver of the car?'

'He stepped straight in without speaking. As far as I remember, the car moved off at once. I imagine it knew where to go. I was looking for a taxi myself, so I did not observe very closely. I am afraid I am not being very helpful, Superintendent.'

'I'm afraid not. I won't keep you any longer. Thank you very much for answering all my questions. There's just one more. I suppose you were present at the performance of Mr Tredegar's Mass. Would you tell me whereabouts you sat in the Hall.'

'Certainly. I think the number was A7—in the front row of the stalls.'

'That was the contralto side, wasn't it? Isn't it a little surprising that someone who can afford to give away fifty guineas to engage a tenor should buy the cheapest seat in order to hear him, when the more expensive seats at the back of the stalls are supposed to be much better?'

'For some people perhaps, but not for me. I have the misfortune to be partially deaf. As it was, I heard only a

143

distorted version of the Mass, but I am afraid it would have been even less satisfactory from a seat further away. Mrs Bainsbury kept this seat for me at my particular request, although she had been anxious to make me a present of one in the Grand Tier.'

'I see,' Simon said doubtfully. 'You don't know the names of anyone in the seats near you, I suppose?'

'Only of one. I gave a seat in the second row to Mary, my maid. She is very much attached to Signor Cassati's voice.'

'I'll have a word with her now, then, and also ask her to show me the typewriter, if I may. I don't think I need to trouble you any further.'

Mrs Sheraton-Smith rang the bell.

'Mary,' she said as the maid appeared, 'before you show the Superintendent out, he would like to see Mr Sheraton-Smith's typewriter. He may also have some questions to ask you. You may come back for the tea tray after he has left.'

Simon chatted to the girl as he was led across a large hall. She was about seventeen, neat and friendly and willing to talk.

'It must be lonely for you, working on your own in a big house like this,' he suggested.

She looked at him wide-eyed.

'Oh, I'm not on my own, you know. There's Cook, and Mrs Jenkins in the mornings for the rough, and Jenkins in the garden. I get as much company as if I were living at home.'

'That's a lot of people just to look after Mrs Sheraton-Smith.'

'Well, she's always had it and you can't expect a lady of her age to start scrubbing her own floors suddenly. She pays good wages and if that's how she likes to spend her money it's not my business to stop her, is it? This is where the typewriter's kept.'

'You like working for her then, do you?' Simon asked, ignoring the machine for the moment.

'Oh, she's ever such a kind mistress. I wouldn't be anywhere else.'

'I hear she gave you a ticket for the concert at which Signor Cassati sang. Did you enjoy it?'

'I thought it was lovely. I'd like to sing in a big choir like that. There are people who say I've got quite a nice voice.'

'Did you notice anything unusual towards the end?'

'You mean before Mr Burr was killed? No, I didn't. I've been trying to think ever since, but I can't. Don't you want to look at the typewriter?'

'Thank you. Is there any paper I could use?'

Mary looked doubtfully in the top drawer of the heavy oak desk.

'I don't know what the right sort of paper is. Would this do? She doesn't use it very often.' She listened for a moment as Simon typed from memory the first paragraph of Mary Smith's letter. 'She's quicker at it than you, all the same, though.'

'Mrs Sheraton-Smith? I thought she didn't type.'

'She doesn't much. But I heard her one day last week and she was fair rattling along.'

'What day last week?'

'It would be Wednesday, because it was while I was still in bed. It was ever so early in the morning. She often gets up early on Wednesdays to go to Early Service, but I'm not expected to be down until seven as usual.'

Simon was excited. He folded the paper neatly into his wallet and hurried away. He could hardly wait while his two specimens were examined but wandered restlessly round his office until the report came up. Mary Smith had typed her letter on Mrs Sheraton-Smith's machine. What was more, she was either a professional typist or at least a practised one—'her effort was much smoother than yours, old man, and it was typed faster than an old-fashioned machine like that will really work'.

Simon ignored the comparison and drove back to the big house in Kensington. Mary opened the door and stared at him in surprise.

145

'Did you forget something?'

'No. I want to see your mistress again. Is she still in?'

'Well, she is, but she's talking to Mrs Bainsbury on the phone and they usually have a long chat. Still, she's an old friend. She won't mind being interrupted.'

'Just a minute.' Simon stepped into the hall and considered. 'I didn't know Mrs Bainsbury was such an old friend. Does she come here at all? Does she ever let herself in? Look, Mary, what I really want to know is this: could it have been her and not Mrs Sheraton-Smith you heard typing last week?'

Mary's face lightened.

'Yes, of course it could. I thought it was funny, Mrs Sheraton-Smith being able to type so fast when she hardly ever does. But Mrs Bainsbury calls for her every Wednesday because they go to the service together. Mrs Sheraton-Smith opens the door and if she isn't quite ready, Mrs Bainsbury waits. And I expect she can type ever so fast because she's some sort of a secretary, isn't she? I'm sure that would be it. She knows where everything's kept. Would you like to ask Mrs Sheraton-Smith about it?'

'I don't think I will come in for the moment, after all. You needn't say that I came again. Thank you very much, Mary; you've been a great help.'

Simon hurried down the steps and walked to another similar building only a few streets away. Here he asked for Mrs Cuthbertson and was shown into a drawing-room almost as cluttered with photographs as Mrs Sheraton-Smith's; in this case, however, the subjects were without exception canine. Simon managed with difficulty to avoid treading on the current member of this doggy procession, a young, lively and extremely objectionable Yorkshire terrier upon which the Metro's ex-chairman kept a motherly eye throughout the interview. Simon's first questions probed Mrs Cuthbertson's dislike of Owen Burr, a dislike which she was quite willing to explain in detail but in which he did not feel any great interest; since the disappearance of Cassati he had become convinced that some more subtle theory was needed to explain Owen's death than that of mere dislike. The purpose of his visit was to collect gossip and towards this he presently turned the conversation.

Mrs Cuthbertson disappointed. Rumour there certainly had been in the past, but fact—that was something on which she refused to commit herself. It might have been true, but equally it might not. It was possible, she would go so far as to say that, it was possible that Mrs Bainsbury had once been the mistress of Evan Tredegar. But that, the Superintendent was to understand, had been thirty years ago, when Mrs Bainsbury was young and unwidowed; the relationship, if it ever existed, might well have ended when she became free to remarry. There were certainly few indications that it still continued; although Mrs Bainsbury's attitude was one of hero-worship, Evan Tredegar's behaviour towards her was offhand to the point sometimes of rudeness. This might be a calculated deception on his part, but it would be such an unnecessary one that it seemed unlikely. It was more probable, was it not, that if the relationship had ever existed, the seventy-nine-year-old man had by now lost interest and would have preferred to forget all about it? Mrs Cuthbertson really couldn't suggest more than that, could she now, Muffin, good doggy, then.

Simon was by now resigned to hearing less than he hoped for; clearly, he would have to approach one of the two principals. In the meantime he went home and opened a tin for dinner.

LATER THE SAME evening he paid a call on Mrs Bainsbury. As his car drew up outside her house it was joined by a taxi from which Evan Tredegar emerged. The two men walked together to the front door, which was opened by Mrs Bainsbury before they had time to ring. She was expecting a visitor, but she was surprised to see Simon and a little doubtful as to what to do with him.

'I'll wait,' announced Tredegar gruffly in the hall. 'Roger will look after me while you get rid of your business. I don't expect you'll be long, will you?'

'I hope not,' Simon answered politely. The Old Man, leaving his heavy coat in a crumpled heap, opened a door opposite to that of the drawing-room.

'Got a chair for me here for ten minutes, Roger? The house is stiff with police wanting to put your mother through the third degree.'

The door closed behind him as Mrs Bainsbury, without speaking, led Simon into her drawing-room.

'I'm sorry to interrupt your evening,' he said apologetically.

'It's all right as long as you don't need to stay too long. We're expecting someone else at eight—someone we're thinking of to take Owen's place. We're more or less going to interview him.'

'I see. I thought perhaps Mr Tredegar's visit was a purely social one. Does he come here often?'

'Very rarely. Only for committee meetings as a rule. Tonight's business is unusual, of course.'

'And yet you are very close friends, are you not?'

'We have known each other for a good many years,' Mrs Bainsbury amended carefully.

Simon drew a deep breath and then stopped to consider again.

'Mrs. Bainsbury,' he said at last, 'I'm about to ask a question which I'm afraid you will consider impertinent, but it is very important, all the same, that you should give me a truthful answer. Has your relationship with Mr. Tredegar ever, at any time, been closer than that of mere friendship?'

She understood what he meant all right; he could tell that

from the blood which flushed her sallow neck. Her face remained pale, however, as she answered him indignantly.

'Your question is unpardonable, and it is completely without foundation. There has never been anything of that sort between us. It is a monstrous suggestion. I cannot imagine how you could have conceived such a notion.'

There was a long pause.

'Well, I'm sorry to hear it,' Simon said at last with all the gravity he could summon. From his wallet he produced the letter signed by Mary Smith and laid it on the table beside his chair, smoothing its creases meticulously before he spoke again. 'I had imagined that your answer, had it been affirmative, might provide a partial explanation of this, but now I must ask you to tell me exactly why you wrote it.' He was not quite certain enough to dare to give her time for denial but pressed on with more confidence than he felt. 'I believe I am right in saying that you typed it last Wednesday morning at the house of your friend, Janet Sheraton-Smith. Before you give me your explanation, I would like to remind you that this letter contains a confession of murder.'

Mrs Bainsbury was very pale.

'Are you accusing me of murder?' she asked tensely.

'I am pointing out that you have yourself admitted to murder. I am suggesting that if you are going to claim that this letter contains a pack of lies, then you would do well to give a truthful explanation of why you sent it to me.'

There was another long, very long, silence.

'It *was* a lie,' she said at last, so softly that Simon could hardly hear. 'I'd been worrying all night, and then I had an opportunity, so I wrote the letter on the spur of the moment. I didn't think there was anything to connect Janet with the case, or that you would ever think to visit her, otherwise I would have waited till I got home. I wrote it because I was sure that Evan could not be a murderer.'

'The law does not very often make mistakes in such a serious matter. If Mr Tredegar is not a murderer, then he is in no danger.'

'How was I to be sure of that? Delia gave me the impression that you were intending to arrest him at any moment.'

'But why should you be so vitally concerned?'

'I suppose that the question you came here tonight to ask was a reasonable one,' Mrs Bainsbury answered after another pause. 'I should not have been so upset by it. It is true that Evan would once have liked me to—well, to do what you were suggesting. That was a long time ago, and I refused. I had a husband, a young son; I was not prepared to risk my domestic happiness for what I thought might be only a flirtation. I didn't find it easy to refuse. I have always had a great admiration for Evan and at that time, when I was still a young woman, I was very much flattered by his interest. But I did refuse, and he was very angry with me. That was the year he wrote his Third Symphony. It was a failure and he blamed me. I blamed myself, too. I have always wanted to be able to do something which would be a recompense for the way in which I felt I had let him down and last week it seemed as if my chance had come. Evan knew nothing about it, of course. I hope it won't be necessary to mention it to him. I'm not sure that he has ever quite forgiven me; it might all be a little embarrassing.'

'I'm afraid I can't promise that. This is a very serious matter, as I am sure you appreciate. I must check it as far as I can.'

There was a ring at the front-door bell. Mrs Bainsbury glanced uncertainly at Simon, who rose to his feet.

'I'll leave you to your business now,' he said. 'I hope you won't interfere any further in mine. It's a dangerous hobby.'

As he went into the hall Roger was just opening the front door. Evan Tredegar, obviously watching for Simon, beckoned him into the little room in which he had been waiting.

'Won't be long,' he shouted across to Mrs Bainsbury. 'Just want a word with the superintendent here.'

The word he wanted was of reassurance. Clearly, he hoped to hear that suspicion had fallen on someone else. Simon was not communicative. He used the brief opportunity for his own purpose. Without revealing the source of his information, he repeated some of the story that Mrs Bainsbury had just told him and asked for comments.

'Pack of lies!' exploded the old man. 'Pack of damned lies. Who the devil spun you a tale like that?'

Roger appeared in the doorway to announce that Mr Tredegar was wanted on the telephone.

'It's Robert Stanley. He says he's been chasing you all round London and that it's urgent.'

He led the way out into the hall and Tredegar followed, shrugging his heavy shoulders at Simon.

'Not the time now. But come up to my flat and I'll let you know about it. Pack of lies! Don't believe a word of it.'

Simon was curious but prepared to wait. The Old Man was clearly in a co-operative and amusing mood. As Simon allowed Roger to show him out, he promised himself a visit to Twickenham the next morning. He did not reflect as he did so that for men in their eightieth year tomorrow does not always come.

CHAPTER SIXTEEN

E ven when next morning Simon found an ambulance standing outside the block of flats in Twickenham it did not immediately occur to him that his journey had already been rendered unprofitable. But when, panting slightly, he had climbed to Evan Tredegar's flat, he found the door standing open, its knocker swathed in a duster and its bell silenced by sticking plaster. In quick alarm Simon stepped into the hall, but at once he had to flatten himself against a wall as two ambulance men appeared carrying a stretcher.

While they negotiated the double corner which made the doorway a difficult one for their burden, Simon had a moment to study the face of Evan Tredegar, all that could be seen above the enswathing blankets. Not a flicker disturbed, not a drop of blood coloured it; the lips, relaxed into a flabby petulance, were blue and the same colour tinged the suddenly thin eyelids which covered the eyes.

The men freed themselves from their difficulty and began a careful descent of the stairs.

'You can go in now,' Annie's voice said tearfully to someone inside the flat. Simon took a step towards it, but at that moment

Dr Smiles appeared, frowning heavily. He recognised Simon with an effort and paused in the doorway.

'What's happened, Doctor? Is he dead?'

'Not quite, Superintendent, but very near. Very near indeed, I'm afraid. Can you wait a moment? I must just see him into the ambulance and have a word with the nurse. Then I'll come back up.'

He did not wait for an answer but disappeared down the stairs in short fussy steps. Simon went into the flat and opened the first door he came to. It was a bedroom in a state of chaos. All three windows were open, and the curtains strained indignantly in the cold December wind. The sheets and blankets from the bed in the centre of the room had been pulled down on to the floor; they lay in a heap on the carpet in front of the gas fire. Beside them stood the doctor's bag and a tray which bore a hypodermic syringe and an assortment of bottles and swabs. A man in dirty blue overalls was crawling round the edge of the floor, leaving behind him a trail of quickly struck and quickly discarded matches.

'What are you doing here?' asked Simon after he had watched this performance for a few seconds. The man straightened himself on his haunches and looked up, unoffended.

'Gas Board,' he said. 'Looking for the leak. But there isn't one, not that I can find. It was the fire all right. Nothing wrong with the tap, either. There's no vent behind the fire, though. People ought to know how dangerous it is, especially when they sleep with their windows shut. Nothing for me to do here.'

He picked up his bag of tools and walked out of the room. Simon followed and was at once caught by Dr Smiles, who guided him towards the study.

'Now then, Superintendent, you want to know what's wrong. He's had a heart attack, either caused by or aggravated by gas poisoning; it's left him completely paralysed. He can breathe and that's all. Can't speak, can't move, can't eat—that's why I've had to get him to hospital, where they can feed him intravenously. Pretty serious at his age, you know. I doubt if he'll ever open his eyes again. A younger man might get something back—speech, a little hand movement—but there's not much hope for a man of seventy-nine with his medical history. I'd give him three days perhaps, not more.'

'Which came first, the heart or the gas?' Simon asked. 'The gas man said it wasn't a leak. Do you think he tried to kill himself?'

'That hadn't even occurred to me, but I suppose it's a possibility. But not a very great one. He wasn't what I'd call a suicidal type and he'd no special worry that I know of. Just a minute, though.' He went to the door and opened it. 'Annie!'

She appeared at once.

'Yes, Doctor.'

'If you know where Mr Tredegar kept his pills, the ones I gave him, bring them along here, will you.'

The maid returned in a moment carrying a small bottle and Dr Smiles shook the contents into his hand.

'Sixteen,' he said. 'It's a week since I gave him twenty and he took one of them at once. That means he's been having a certain amount of trouble with his heart, but it seems reasonable. These are to quieten the heart down, but they have a fairly knock-out effect. You could do yourself a lot of damage with ten of them. I wouldn't have given him so many if I hadn't been sure that he was a man who liked living. If he turned on the gas deliberately, he'd have taken some of these first—and then made himself comfortable in bed. Very nice too; I'll do it myself one of these days. I'm sure it was an accident.'

'How would it have happened in that case?'

'Too easy. He stoops to turn on the fire, has a heart attack and collapses before he has time to light it. Or, as he was wearing his night clothes, he may have been stooping to turn it off, and then hit the tap as he fell.'

'In that case the fire would still be hot and would relight itself, I imagine,' Simon suggested.

'Well, then you can have it the other way round. He doesn't turn the fire off properly for some reason, wakes up in the middle of the night, finds the room full of gas, which has already affected him, gets out to turn it off and collapses then. That fits in very well with the way the bedclothes have been dragged down with him, but not with the fact that the windows were closed. I know that he always sleeps with them open, although in weather like this he may shut them while he undresses.'

'There's no explanation that fits with quite everything, is there?' said Simon thoughtfully. 'Is there any chance of asking him about it?'

'You can ask, and he may understand you, but he won't be able to answer. Not at the moment, anyway. In a day or two, if he's still alive, he may be able to flicker an eyelid at you. But don't rely on it. He's a dying man, I'm afraid. I must get down to the hospital now. Goodbye.'

When he had gone Simon returned to the bedroom where Annie, to his annoyance, had finished making the bed and was dusting the furniture, sniffing as she went.

'This must have been a great shock to you, Annie.'

'Oh, it was, sir. I found him and all.'

'Tell me all about it. What time did you find him?'

'Half-past nine, it was. I come at half-past eight, but I've got orders not to disturb him. He rings when he wants his breakfast and often it's not before ten. But today I smelt the gas when I was polishing the corridor outside his door, so I went in.'

She began to cry again.

'Where did you find him?'

'Down by the gas fire, just where he was when the doctor came. I tried to move him, but he was too heavy, so I just had to open the windows and flap the air round instead.'

'You've got a key of your own, I suppose. Do you know if anyone else has one?'

'I don't think so, except of course the person who stole the mortice key. And that's no good now, because the lock's been changed.'

Simon nodded reflectively and leaned out of one of the open windows of the bedroom. There was a right-angled turn in the wall within a yard of the end one and another window faced it diagonally about three feet away.

'Where does that window belong?' he asked, pointing. 'Is it somewhere in the flat?'

Annie came closer to have a look.

'No, that's in the corridor outside. Shall I show you?'

Simon followed her and pushed open the window he had seen, which was situated on the top landing of the staircase.

'Anyone can walk up here without being noticed, I suppose ?'

'The porter might see them during the day. He's supposed to stay in the hall until ten o'clock. But I think he often knocks off a bit earlier for a drink. Nobody wants him at that hour, so it doesn't matter. Still, the murderer couldn't jump from that window to Mr Tredegar's, could he?'

'Why not? It looks dangerous because it's so high. But if it were on the ground you could do it easily. Even here it only needs a head for heights.' He pulled the window down and turned to stare at her. 'What do you mean by saying "the murderer"?'

'Well, of course, I know he isn't dead. I meant the person who tried to murder him.'

'But why do you think it wasn't an accident?'

'Doesn't seem likely it would be an accident, does it, with all the queer things that have been going on?'

'Come inside the flat,' said Simon. 'Now tell me, what *has* been going on?'

'Well, there was that key being stolen, and now money gone, and the secret visitors.'

'We know all about the key now, so you needn't worry about that. Tell me about the money.'

'It was three hundred pounds. Mr Tredegar brought it back from the bank yesterday afternoon. He showed me where he put it—a big wad of notes, it was—so that I wouldn't leave any strangers alone in the study. It was in the second drawer of his desk and he locked it and put the key in his pocket. Then this morning, when I was dusting, I saw that the key was back in the drawer, so I opened it and the money wasn't there. I didn't think anything of it at the time, of course, but then I found Mr Tredegar so I realised it must have been burglars. Perhaps they had a fight.'

'I think the doctor would have noticed that, Annie. Tell me about the secret visitors. Who were they?'

'They wouldn't be secret if I knew, would they?' said Annie. 'It was only one, really. Somebody had a glass of port with Mr Tredegar last night. He's not supposed to, either; the doctor said so.'

'But that needn't have been a secret. If Mr Tredegar hadn't been taken ill, he would probably have told you all about it.'

'Then why did he wash up the glasses himself? It's not a thing he ever does. He knows I don't mind finding a bit of washing-up when I come in the morning.'

'Are you sure that he did?'

'Either him or the visitor. All covered with bits of fluff from the cloth they were and standing the right way up instead of upside down like I always put them.'

'I'd like to see them,' said Simon.

'They're in the kitchen. Of course, I've washed them up properly by now.'

Simon stopped walking.

'In that case I'm not interested after all. I think I'll have a

157

look at Mr Tredegar's diary. I suppose his suit will still be in the bedroom. You get on with your work, then, Annie. I can find my way.'

The diary page for the previous day was blank but a glance back showed that the book was used more for musical notes than as a record of engagements. The bedroom, thoroughly searched, was equally empty of the missing £300; Simon phoned the Old Man's bank manager and was lucky. The notes had been new and within half an hour he was able to circulate their numbers. He could only hope, as he walked back to the office, that the recipient or thief would not take too long to dispose of his haul. On his desk, however, was a note which made him temporarily forget all about Evan Tredegar and his visitors. It read only: 'Come and see me. We're on to it. Bill.'

CHAPTER SEVENTEEN

Simon found Bill preparing to leave his office.

'You're only just in time. If you want a joy ride, get your coat and come. We've found your puddle.'

Simon looked blank for a moment and Bill explained condescendingly.

'Remember that little story about a Famous Missing Person and a Daimler that you slid so happily on to my desk. Well, we've found the puddle where the Daimler picked up its splashes. Or rather, the boys down in Kent have, and we're just off to tell them if they've been clever. Coming?'

'Twenty seconds,' said Simon and ran for his coat and gloves. When they were in the car he asked, 'How do you know it's right?'

'We don't know for certain, of course. But you know how wet it was on Christmas Eve and how frosty it's been ever since. Well, they've found some frozen tyre-marks that check with the Daimler's and have no business to be where they are. One of the tyres, luckily, is a new one which doesn't match with the other three, so they're not likely to have made a mistake. Distance is all right for that mileage, too.'

'Where are they?'

'Off a private road just outside Bexley. There's a wood on one side of this road which belongs to some local big-bug called Sir Joshua Mester and it's preserved. Apparently, he asked the station whether they could send a man on beat down this road occasionally; his own man is ill and some of his birds had been driven off by a car that had backed on to the private part of his land to turn. We'd sent our details round, of course, and the man who went out, bless his bright soul, made a note of the tracks and thought of us at once. Pretty smart work, actually, although I hate to let them know it.'

'And what are we going to find when we get there?'

'Well, personally I'm expecting to find a body, but you're the one who knows.'

'Yes,' said Simon slowly. 'I'm expecting to find a body too.'

They found the place where the Daimler had turned easily enough; it was guarded by two young policemen who were determined not to be sent away now that the exciting part of the job was due to begin. Their help was accepted; the ground was so hard that nothing could obliterate the tracks already made, so while Simon searched for footprints the other three men began a general scrutiny of the ground. It was they who made the first discovery—an empty but labelled bottle which had held chloroform, thrown into the undergrowth. As they wrapped it up carefully and put it in the car, they heard a crash and an oath. Quickly they followed the sound and discovered Simon picking himself up from what, judging by his expression, had been a heavy fall.

'Why didn't you tell me about the elephant pits?' he demanded morosely of the local men; following his eyes they saw with consternation the deep, narrow hole into which he had so nearly stepped. Bill peered down it curiously and kicked a stone from the edge; there was a long wait before he heard the brisk smack as it hit the hard bottom.

'Must be the best part of forty feet,' he said. 'What the heck is it?'

One of the local men answered.

'It's a dene-hole, sir. You're quite right, we should have warned you. There are a lot of them in this part of the world, although I didn't know there were any actually in this wood.'

'But what are they?' asked Simon, who had now recovered from the shock of feeling nothingness under his feet. 'Are they natural?'

'I don't think anybody knows, sir, My father once told me that the Ancient Britons dug them out and used them for grain storage, but if that's true I don't see how they'd get the grain out again. I have heard other theories too—either that they were once used as prisons or that warriors used to put their women down there while they were away from home. They're very dangerous now, anyhow. We get a lot of accidents—dogs mainly, but sometimes small boys. When they're on private land, and the only people who are likely to fall in are trespassers, we can't force the landowner to cover them.'

Bill and Simon looked at each other, the same thought in each mind.

'Take the car and get back to Bexley,' said Simon. 'Come back with ropes and torches—in fact, bring a couple of firemen and their equipment with you. I expect they're used to this sort of job.'

'Yes, sir. We brought spades with us, sir.'

'Bad luck,' said Simon. 'Never mind. We may need them later on.'

He watched the car drive away and turned to the remaining young constable.

'Before they come back, we'd better see how many of these holes there are. If we assume that Cassati was unconscious when he arrived here—and that bottle is fairly good evidence—then we may also assume that the driver wouldn't want to drag such a heavy burden further than he could help. I'll take this section, you stay in the middle, and Bill, you have a look on the left, will you?'

The three men pushed their way through the undergrowth systematically. By the time the firemen arrived Simon could feel tolerably certain that there were not more than three dene-holes in the neighbourhood, besides the one into which he himself had almost fallen.

The examination was quick and efficient. It was possible to inspect the emptiness of two of the holes by the light of powerful lamps lowered to the bottom. The other two each had a more impenetrable shape, resembling that of an hourglass. But even at the narrowest point there was room for a man to descend. The only body which was brought to the surface was that of a fox.

The firemen returned to their station. Simon and Bill looked at each other in disappointment.

'There's this,' said Bill, without expectation.

He led the way to a part of the wood which he had been examining. A path ran through it, well-marked with footprints of which Simon could make nothing. In a clearing a small trench had been dug, to a depth of about a foot. It was difficult to see what its purpose could be and there was no corresponding mound nearby. The earth had been darkened by frost so that there was no means of telling whether its disturbance were recent. They stared at it for a moment in silence. Bill prodded it with his stick, but it was rock-hard.

'We can't ask anyone to start digging on spec until there's a thaw,' he said gloomily. 'We seem to have drawn a blank. Do you think there's any point in searching the rest of the wood?'

'Cassati would have been a frightful weight to drag,' Simon answered with an equal lack of enthusiasm. 'And we've covered a pretty wide area in detail. We might have a quick look round the rest, but I don't think there's much hope.'

His lack of faith was justified; they found nothing suspicious.

'I'll have to leave it to you,' Simon said at last. 'As soon as the thaw arrives get as many of the Bexley police as you can and give this semi-circle round the tyre-tracks a digging over. We must be near the answer, if we could only be a little more clever about seeing it.'

'When you find the body, what's it going to prove for you?' Bill asked curiously.

Simon laughed shortly.

'Heaven knows. Perhaps only that I'm looking for a madman who becomes homicidal every time he hears sweet music. Music's the only link I can find between the two of them—or perhaps three now, with Evan Tredegar. I'd better get back now and see how he is. I've put a man in his room, but, if he does recover his speech, I'd like to be there myself.'

They drove back together in silence. Simon was dropped at the hospital, where he learned that there had been no change at all, for better or worse, in Evan Tredegar's condition. Thoughtfully he made his way to Twickenham. He had an excuse now as well as an opportunity to examine the composer's private papers. A search warrant might have caused trouble; now no one was likely to worry if he acted without one.

Annie certainly made no difficulty; clearly, she was glad to have the company of someone she knew. Simon went into the study and settled down to a systematic examination of all its owner's papers. After two hours he had had enough. There was plenty here to interest a musician but nothing for a detective. He phoned Sergeant Flint to see whether anything important had come in during the day and then cursed himself for not having done this earlier, for he learned that at half-past ten that morning the three hundred-pound notes missing from Evan Tredegar's drawer had been paid into Shirley Marsden's account by that young lady herself.

Simon left at once and within twenty minutes had arrived at

Shirley's flat. He found her busily working on Owen's book and came to the point at once.

'Have you heard the news about Evan Tredegar?'

She smiled happily.

'Yes, it is good, isn't it?' Then a slight frown wrinkled her forehead. 'But how did you hear? It's early yet for it to have been announced.'

'I think perhaps we have different pieces of news in mind,' Simon said after a moment of surprise. 'What were you thinking of?'

'I thought you were talking about the Old Man's knighthood, but it isn't official until Friday, of course.'

'Oh, you knew about that, did you?'

'Yes, he told Owen and me about it as soon as he heard, under strict oaths of secrecy. I think he would have burst if he couldn't have told someone, the pet. What's your news, though, if it isn't that?'

'I'm afraid my news is that Evan Tredegar is dying.'

Shirley half rose to her feet, then slowly sat down again. After a moment's silence she looked up at Simon.

'Is he dying naturally—I mean, because he's old?' she asked quietly. 'Or has he been shot too?'

'He hasn't been shot. As to whether it's natural, I'm hoping you may be able to help me there. I think you may have been the last person to see him alive.'

She did not attempt to deny this and there was no look of surprise on her face as she considered.

'He seemed perfectly normal and well when I left him. I didn't notice anything unusual at all.'

'What time was that?'

'About a quarter to ten. I was there for less than an hour.'

'Did you have anything to drink while you were there?'

'He offered me port, but I don't like it, so I didn't; he didn't drink anything either.'

'Did you know that he suffered from heart trouble?'

'Not until the day he couldn't conduct the Mass. He told me after that. Is that what's wrong?'

'It may be, but I'm not sure yet. Would you mind telling me why you visited him last night? Was it your idea or his?'

'His, entirely. I'd been talking to him about Owen's book on the phone yesterday morning—I asked him if he would write an Introduction, as a matter of fact. He seemed very interested and invited me round. When I got there, he asked whether I'd found a publisher yet. I said I hadn't and told him that there might be some difficulty—it isn't a book that will sell well, of course, and when the author's already dead the publisher doesn't even have the hope of a more popular work to come. The Old Man didn't seem surprised. He fished in his drawer and produced a wad of notes. He said he'd like the book to be published, and, if I had any difficulty, he'd like me to be able to offer to pay for it myself. He didn't let me say anything after that—said he didn't want the money back whatever happened and that if I had a proper offer for the manuscript, I could keep this as payment for my work on it. It had already occurred to me that I might have to pay for the book and I've only got my allowance, so I accepted it.'

'How much did he give you?'

'Three hundred pounds. I counted it as soon as I got home. Do you think he knew he was going to be ill? That would explain why he was in such a hurry to give me the money. When he first offered it, I suggested that he should wait until I knew whether the money would be wanted, and how much, but he insisted on my having it at once.'

'Did he mention what he was proposing to do when you left? Did he say anything about going to bed?'

'No. He usually goes to bed quite late. I don't think he needs much sleep. He told me once that all his best work was done after midnight.'

'He didn't mention that he was expecting any other callers?'

'No.'

Simon looked at her sharply. Her negative might be true, but he was certain that she had intended to add something to it and had only changed her mind at the last minute. He waited for a moment in silence, but she did not take the opportunity to add anything.

'Did you meet anyone on the stairs as you left?'

'No.'

Again there was the slight hesitation, the sudden dropping of the eyes.

'Did you by any chance wash up two glasses during your visit last night?'

Shirley looked relieved at what seemed to be a change in his approach.

'Certainly not. He's got a maid—and anyway, as I said, we didn't have anything to drink.'

She waited for the next question, but Simon's attention had been distracted by a book which lay on the arm of a chair. Its title was simply *Kent*, and although it had the appearance of a book which had been read, it was obviously a new one.

'Are you interested in Kent?' he asked idly.

'My home's there. I know it quite well. I wouldn't have bought that myself, but it's nice to have as a present. I haven't read it yet, though.'

'It looks as though it has been read.'

She laughed.

'I always read books myself before I give them away, I'm afraid. I don't mind at all if John does too.'

'John Southerley?'

'Yes. He brought it round yesterday.'

'Where is your home?'

'Bexley. I don't expect you know it. It was a nice village once, but it's spoilt now.'

'Did you spend Christmas there?'

'Yes. I go home most weekends. My mother grumbles if I don't.'

'I suppose you know all about dene-holes, then?'

'There's one in the wood at the bottom of our garden. I believe it caused my parents a lot of anxiety when I was small.'

'I wonder if the book mentions them. I'm rather interested in the subject.'

He searched in the index and found, to his great delight, a map which showed the position of all the known holes. The roads marked were unnamed, however, and he appealed to Shirley for help.

'Can you tell from this which of the holes are on Sir Joshua Mester's land?'

She came closer to look.

'Well, that's his house there,' she pointed. 'I'm not sure about the boundary of his land. These fields would certainly be his, and this wood.'

Simon ran his finger along a thin line.

'Then this would be a sort of private road.'

'That's right.'

He knew where he was now and stared at the map. Just off the road lay a cluster of five of the little circles which represented the ancient holes.

'I've been a fool,' he announced to the surprised Shirley. 'I must get back. Before I go, will you just confirm that it was John Southerley you saw last night somewhere near the Old Man's flat?'

She was not a good liar and she could not make herself deny it. Seeing that he had read her silence, she apologised for it.

'I didn't actually see him,' she said, justifying her previous answers. 'But when I left the block of flats, I did notice John's car standing outside. There wasn't anyone in it.'

As Simon left, he noticed that the sun was shining; the thaw had begun.

CHAPTER EIGHTEEN

'If I'd had any sense at all,' said Simon, 'it might have occurred to me that if one finds a hole that has been dug without any sign of the earth has that been taken from it, there's a chance that the earth has been put down another hole. Anyway, the cold weather seems to have broken now. The Bexley men can start digging first thing tomorrow. They can get the position from a map and light a couple of bonfires to help the sun. But tell them to go carefully and not to touch the body until they've got a doctor handy. If they let me know as soon as they're sure they're on the right track, I'll come down at once.'

Bill nodded and made a note.

'Mind you,' he said. 'I don't reckon this is my business really. It's time I handed the whole thing over to you Murder people. You can't call a body a Missing Person.'

'Well, you haven't found him yet,' answered Simon reasonably enough. 'But from tomorrow morning I will take personal responsibility. Just at the moment I've got some very important business to deal with.'

'I know,' said Bill, grinning all over his face. 'I saw her arrive.

But from the look on her face I should have thought that she was going to deal with you.'

'What on earth—My God!' said Simon, looking in horror at his watch. 'Delia!'

He rushed back to his room, pursued by the echoes of Bill's laughter. Delia was patiently reading a magazine. She looked up calmly as he burst in.

'Only fifty minutes late! I'm sorry if it's not done for me to come here, but the waiter was beginning to look disbelieving and the smells were making me very hungry. When I asked for you, I tried my best to look as if I had a confession of murder in my handbag. Didn't fool your sergeant for a moment, though. He's obviously used to showing young ladies into the sanctum.'

'Darling, I'm so sorry. I can't believe it's nearly seven. I haven't even had lunch yet. I always seem to be asking you to forgive me. May I again?'

'This is one of the easier occasions. I'm only sorry you're having to work so hard. Will you be able to get away this evening?'

'I'll come now, as soon as I've tidied up these papers. I had meant to see John Southerley before I knocked off, but he can wait until tomorrow.'

'What's he been doing? Is he still on your list of suspects?'

'Getting higher on it, I'm afraid. You see, it's pretty certain that Cassati has been murdered—we should know tomorrow. It's not really very likely that it should only be a coincidence, the murder of two musicians within a week; there's a strong proba-bility that the same man was responsible for both. One of the best reasons why Cassati should have been killed would be if he knew the identity of Owen's murderer. Now just look at this.' He spread out on the desk the plan of the Festival Hall which Delia had already seen on the night of the concert. 'We already know that John was furiously angry with Owen. We also know that the gun was at some point in his possession. Suppose that in the moment after he finished playing, he pulled it out and shot Owen, who would be most likely to notice?' Simon jabbed with his pencil at the two squares he had drawn next to the larger shape of the piano. 'The bass and tenor. They could hardly help seeing anything unusual.'

'Has anything happened to the bass?'

'I checked on him. He left for America on Boxing Day, for a tour. I couldn't find anything to link him with Owen, so I didn't bother much about him. Anyway, he may not have noticed anything, while Cassati may have shown by some movement that *he* had.'

'Why wait so long to get rid of him, in that case? He might have phoned the police at any moment.'

'Lack of opportunity would explain the delay in killing. Cassati didn't go out much and when he did, except on concert nights, his valet was always with him. As for his silence, anyone might be chary of getting mixed up with the police in a strange country.'

'Then it wasn't necessary to kill him.'

'The murderer wouldn't dare not to be sure. Anyway, it was certainly a man who drove Cassati out to his death, if he is dead, and it was someone fit who got into the Old Man's bedroom last night.' This part was news to Delia, and he gave her the details briefly. 'And John was in Twickenham last night. It *may* have been a coincidence, but…'

'But why should he want to hurt the Old Man? I don't see how that fits in.'

'Nor do I at the moment, but I don't pretend to know the whole story. By the way, do you know anything about a place called Bexley?'

'Well, Shirley Marsden used to live there before she took her London flat. I spent a weekend at her parents' house there once, with Mrs Bainsbury and Roger—about three years ago. Why?'

'Oh, nothing in particular.'

Delia was silent, staring at the diagram. She picked up a ruler and laid it across the paper, first in one position and then in another. Simon, glancing hastily through a memorandum which had arrived during the afternoon, paid no attention until suddenly she drew in her breath sharply.

'Simon! Oh, Simon, what a fool you've been—what a fool everyone's been. Just look at this.'

There was a knock on the door and after a discreet pause Sergeant Flint's head appeared.

'A Mr John Southerley would like to see you, sir.'

Simon's eyebrows rose.

'Show him in. Isn't it time you went home?'

'Just off, sir.'

John looked pale, thought Delia, and under the determined good humour of his voice he was angry.

'I believe you want to speak to me.'

'How did you know that?'

'Shirley phoned me half an hour ago. She was rather incoherent, but the gist of her remarks seemed to be that I was about to be accused of poisoning the Old Man. If I may say so very politely, I would prefer it if you would discuss your strange theories with me before you start broadcasting them among people whose good opinion I value.'

'I certainly made no mention of poison to Miss Marsden; the thought never occurred to me.'

'She can hardly have invented the whole incident. You may not have made any specific accusation, but she is not insensitive. I gather that drinks and washed-up glasses were a feature of your conversation.'

'Would you like me to go?' asked Delia, acutely embarrassed. 'I can wait downstairs.'

'Not on my account,' said John. 'All I propose to say is that last night I had a glass of port from a decanter produced by

Evan Tredegar and poured out by Evan Tredegar and that I drank it. I did not wash up my glass and my host was in the best of health when I left him.'

'What time was that?' asked Simon.

'About half-past eleven. I didn't notice particularly.'

'And what time did you arrive?'

'I knocked on the door at ten o'clock precisely, the time for which I was invited.'

'Oh, you went by invitation.'

'I did, at some inconvenience to myself.'

'And what was the purpose of the invitation?'

'To try out a suite for piano that the Old Man had been working on. He's not much of an instrumentalist and he can't cope with his own difficult bits. He sent me the manuscript score on Saturday and asked me to come over last night, to play it through and give him any comments I might have from the pianist's point of view. Which I did. It wasn't very good.'

'How is it that you didn't meet Miss Marsden on the stairs, since she saw your car outside the flats?'

'I was in the pub opposite, waiting till ten o'clock. I was always taught that it wasn't polite to arrive early.'

'Do you know Kent well, Mr Southerley?'

'Not at all. Unless Folkestone's in Kent; perhaps it is. I used to spend holidays there as a child.'

'Where did you live as a child?'

'Kilburn.'

'With your parents?'

'Of course.'

'Are they still alive?'

'No.'

'But you knew them—they didn't die when you were very young or anything like that?'

'My father was killed in the war when I was young; my mother died five years ago.'

'Do you know whether there was any physical resemblance between you and your father?'

'I have no idea.'

'But you have no doubt that your mother's husband was your father?'

John exploded.

'Are all policemen as bloody impertinent as you? My mother was my mother and my father was my father, and, if you don't believe me, I presume you know how to look it up. I came here because I thought I might be of some help to you, but I'm damned if I'm going to sit here while you insult me. Goodnight, Delia. Forgive me if I don't fall for your boyfriend.'

He slammed out of the door. Simon made no effort to detain him.

'He takes offence easily, doesn't he?'

'Well, darling, I think you *were* pretty offensive,' Delia said warmly. 'And you must admit that his story was reasonable.'

'Well,' said Simon mildly, 'I didn't expect him to come here especially to confess to murder. He's had time to think about it; there's no reason why he shouldn't be able to produce something that hangs together. He's answered my questions, but the answers don't change any of my reasons for needing to ask. So what is a bloody impertinent policeman to do?'

'Well, he *could* decide that he hasn't had any lunch and that the question could be equally well discussed over dinner.'

'You're quite right,' said Simon. 'Case dismissed. In the ordinary course of events murderers wait until we catch up with them. This case is only disturbing because one wonders who's going to be eliminated from the scene next. However, we should have a few days before the next elimination, judging by progress so far. Dinner ho! I'll take the first course here, if I may.'

He came over to kiss her, pushing the murder of Owen Burr to the back of his mind. And although Delia applied a good many epithets to her escort during the course of the evening, she did not remember again to tell him exactly why he had been a fool.

CHAPTER NINETEEN

At ten o'clock next morning Simon stood on the edge of the fifth dene-hole. It had been emptied of the earth which had completely filled the top three feet and now two men were working with ropes and hooks to dislodge a large piece of wood, presumably resting on a natural ledge, which still blocked their view of the bottom.

'I see what happened.' Simon turned to the police doctor who stood next to him, a slim figure dressed at the moment in a fireman's overalls. 'It must be another of these hourglass holes. He pushes Cassati down, either dead or alive, blocks the opening with a piece of tree trunk and shovels earth on top so that we don't notice—and so that nothing will be heard, presumably. That means there must have been a certain amount of air down there. If he was alive when he went in, do you think there's any hope for him now?'

The doctor hardly paused to consider.

'Five days and six nights without food, water, light or fresh air—or hope; a professional escapologist might just survive it, but not an ordinary man. Certainly he wouldn't be sane, and I shall be very surprised if he's been dead for less than three days. But I'll go down before he's moved, just in case.'

The wood came away suddenly, pitching one of the two workers flat on his back. There was a scampering of earth falling to the bottom of the deep narrow hole and then silence. Simon called down, but there was no reply. Torches were lowered. Everything seemed brown and earthy, but suddenly Simon drew in his breath, almost certain that he had caught a glimpse of black and white. He nodded to the doctor, who had already slipped into a wire cradle. There was another slip-fall of earth while the men on the surface strained against the pull of the wire rope; then a few minutes' silence and at last a shout.

'All right. Pull up carefully.'

It seemed to Simon hours before the body of Cassati finally lay on the ground. To the doctor, waiting in the darkness with earth cascading down on top of him as the heavy load was eased with difficulty through the narrowest part of the opening, the time must have appeared endless. While he waited for the second ascent, Simon had time to study the unpleasant sight before him.

Cassati was not only dead but messily dead. His clothes were covered with dirt, but this did not hide the expression on his face. His left arm was fastened tightly to his body by thin wire which encircled him ten or eleven times; clearly, he had struggled against it, for it had cut through his clothes to the flesh. The right arm was also pinned down by the wire, but in this case the encircling bands stopped above the elbow. For some reason he had been free to move the lower part of the arm and the right hand and wrist. More surprisingly still, the right hand clasped a dagger, the point broken and the remaining part of the blade covered with dried blood. Cassati's legs had also been tied together with the same cutting thin wire, but only as far as the knee, so that he would still presumably have been able to take short steps.

With a pant of exertion the doctor reached the surface and freed himself of the line. He came straight over to join Simon.

'I can tell you one thing at once,' he said. 'This man was not only alive but conscious when he fell. For one thing, he's broken his hip in a way which would be less likely if he were inert and, for another, he seems to have clung for a moment with his right hand to a bit of root, until it broke away. There are definite marks where he kicked into the sides of the hole in an effort to push himself up again. In that position they couldn't have been caused by anything else.'

'Cause of death?' asked Simon, as a matter of routine.

The doctor continued his examination of the body for several minutes before he answered.

'Here,' he said at last. Simon leaned across to see. Beneath the dirt on Cassati's left side, his clothes were heavily stained with blood. It had flowed from a gash in the left wrist. The doctor slipped his finger between the wrist and the body.

'The artery was cut after he'd been fastened like this; otherwise the cut would certainly have been made right across the wrist instead of from one side to the middle, which is all that could be reached in this position. It was almost certainly self-inflicted, with this dagger, after the point had broken. It broke while he was down there; I found the other piece and it's pretty plain how it snapped and what it was used for. Even with a broken hip he must have been conscious while he was down there and quite aware of what was going to happen. It looks as though he started off by trying to carve steps in the wall. The slope was against him for that, though; the walls bulge outwards for about six feet from the bottom. Then he tried to hack out a tunnel—or perhaps the idea was that by cutting earth away from the wall he could raise his standing level. Perhaps the frost stopped that, or just general weakness. Anyway, my guess is that he realised he was finished and decided to speed the process up a little. To answer your question, I can't say exactly until I've made a proper examination, but loss of blood is the most likely reason.'

Simon was feeling slightly sick; he nodded without speaking and went to give instructions to the driver of the ambulance which was already waiting. There was one more unpleasant task to be done first, however; with distaste Simon emptied the dead man's pockets. A first glance suggested that most of the papers in them would be in Italian, a language with which he was unacquainted, and he put them away for the moment. The wire would almost certainly be untraceable, but the dagger might provide a clue; before he levered open Cassati's stiff fingers, however, he tried some experiments with his own right arm, holding the elbow closely to his side. The doctor watched curiously.

'I was wondering where the dagger came from,' Simon explained. 'Unless he kept it in his breast pocket—which seems a curious habit—I don't see that he could have reached it after he was tied up, do you? Yet if he had managed to get it free before he was tied, he would have been able to protect himself. In any case, why did his attacker leave one hand free, and why not take the dagger away?'

He ran his fingers round inside the breast pocket. It contained no sheath, but there was no cut in the cloth to suggest that a sharp weapon had been clumsily drawn from it.

'Perhaps he found the dagger at the bottom of the hole,' suggested the doctor helpfully.

'Then why should his right hand have been left so considerately free to pick it up? I can understand the legs; presumably he was made to go from the car to here under his own steam. But the hand?'

'Doesn't it suggest that the murderer made him a present of the dagger and gave him the opportunity to use it—hoping perhaps that if he was caught, he could claim the death to be a suicide and not murder.'

'He'd surely have untied his victim in that case before pushing him down. Anyway, I can't imagine that anyone who was subtle enough to think of that as a possible defence would be sufficiently half-witted to believe it.'

'Well, luckily that's the sort of thing I don't have to worry about. I'll do the post-mortem this afternoon and let you have a report at once.'

He nodded in a friendly way and went off to the ambulance. Simon, returning by car in less gruesome company, studied the papers which he had taken from Cassati's pockets. There was more than he would have expected a man to carry about in evening dress, but he was chiefly interested in one thing—the name of Owen Burr—so he was able to skim through the Italian, hoping that those two words would stand out to cheer him; somewhere, surely, there must be a link between the two deaths. The only reference, however, to Owen was contained in a cutting from *The Times*, whose musical critic considered at length the merits of Evan Tredegar's composition and welcomed the tenor's contribution in glowing terms. The notice ended:

'The performance was ably and, in the faster passages, brilliantly conducted by Mr Owen Burr, whose tragic death at its conclusion is a great loss to the musical world of the future.'

— NEWS REPORT: PAGE 6.

'Not much there,' thought Simon, and continued his search. At the bottom of the pile was a folded sheet of paper which, he remembered, he had found alone in a trouser pocket. It was a letter, and the address at its head was familiar; so too, fortunately, was the language in which it was written.

Dear Sr Cassati (it read),

179

I am anxious to speak to you before you leave England on a matter of some personal importance to you. I shall therefore call at your dressing-room after the performance tonight and hope that you may be able to give me a few moments of your attention. I think that my name—or rather, that of my late son—may not be unfamiliar to you.

Yours faithfully,
  Janet Sheraton-Smith.

Simon leaned forward and gave his driver new instructions. Ten minutes later the car drew up outside Mrs Sheraton-Smith's house in Kensington and was dismissed. Mary opened the door in her working clothes, looking a little more untidy than her afternoon self but no less pretty.

'Mrs Sheraton-Smith doesn't usually see visitors in the morning,' she said doubtfully. 'She is in, though, and I suppose you're different. Will you wait a minute?'

He waited longer but at last he was shown into a smaller room than the over-decorated drawing-room. Mrs Sheraton-Smith was sitting at a small writing desk. She motioned Simon to a chair but made no pretence of being pleased to see him. He wondered for a moment how to begin and his first question was intended to startle.

'Mrs Sheraton-Smith,' he said. 'Why did you hate Owen Burr so much?'

He had failed. The heavy, over-powdered face stared at him impassively.

'I think you have made a mistake, Superintendent. I did not hate Owen Burr at all.'

He tried for a moment to out-stare her, to call her bluff, and then like a revelation there came to him the enormity of his own stupidity, the significance of his own diagram, the importance of the remark which Delia had forgotten to repeat.

Of course, he realised incredulously, Owen was only a

mistake. He turned at the wrong time and suddenly, but it was Cassati all the time.

Relief flooded over him, relief that the impossible link need no longer be found, together with indignation that he should have wasted so much time on people who were no longer of any importance. He looked up, almost smiling at the comparative simplicity of his present task Mrs. Sheraton-Smith was watching him unemotionally and waiting.

'Is that all you wanted to ask me?' she said at last.

'I'm sorry. It was the wrong question. What I should have said was this: why did you hate Cassati so much?'

'That is a question, I am afraid, which I am not able to answer.'

'I will ask another, then. You told me before that you had no particular memory of your conversation with Cassati on Christmas Eve. But I have a letter here which suggests that the subject you wished to discuss was an important one. Can I persuade you to remember a little more now?'

'I am afraid not. The subject of the intended conversation was a private one and it was never adequately dealt with. I did not realise when I wrote the letter which you are holding how public a singer's dressing-room is.'

'You mention your son in this letter. In what way was he connected with Cassati?'

She looked down for a moment before she answered; clearly, she was emotionally affected by the reference. But her voice, when she spoke, was calm and controlled.

'All the questions you have asked are the same question, Superintendent, and the answer to them all is the same. It is one which I am not prepared to give.'

'May I ask why not?'

'I do not wish to cause—embarrassment.'

'To Signor Cassati?'

She was silent.

'If it is his feelings you are thinking of, then I should tell you that he no longer needs your silence. We found his body this morning. He had been most unpleasantly murdered.'

'I see.' She was breathing deeply and abruptly she pushed her chair back and rose to stand at the window. 'I must blame myself very deeply. But it was not an easy thing that I had to do.'

'It is your duty now, Mrs Sheraton-Smith, to answer my questions.'

'I understand that. And now, of course, it can do no harm. The answer to all your questions, Superintendent, is this: I had a son, Geoffrey, who died three days before his twenty-first birthday. He died in Italy during the war, but he was not killed in battle. He was murdered—unpleasantly murdered, I believe your phrase was—by this Signor Cassati.'

CHAPTER TWENTY

Mrs Sheraton-Smith's voice trembled as she spoke, and she raised her hands to her eyes. Her back was still turned to Simon; he waited a moment before he asked his next question.

'If it doesn't distress you too much, I would be most grateful if you would give me some details. How was your son killed, for example?'

'I cannot be exact. It is possible that he was buried alive. It is also possible that he was flogged to death, or that he died by his own hand to avoid either of these fates.'

Mrs Sheraton-Smith was near to collapse, but Simon went stolidly on.

'Would he have the means to do that?'

'That is what this Cassati tried to make them do—there were several of them; Geoffrey was not the only one—and so he gave them the means. Each of these boys was made to crawl to his grave and crouch on hands and knees at the bottom, where he was covered first with a plank and then with earth; I suppose there would be enough air to keep him alive for a short while. If he refused to move, he was flogged until he was unconscious and then flogged again as soon as he came to his senses, over and over again. But he was given a knife, with which he could stab himself if he wished to speed his death. What sort of a madness was it, Superintendent, that could inflict on boys of twenty such agony of mind, forcing them to cut off with their own hands the life which was only just beginning for them?' She broke down completely; Simon rose hurriedly and helped her to a chair, but she refused his suggestion of a drink.

'I must apologise. I thought I had faced this and accepted it, but it is a terrible thing to know about one's own son, that he should have suffered so much.'

'I am very sorry that I should have to ask you to talk about it. Where did all this take place?'

'In a prisoner-of-war camp in the north of Italy; I can give you the address. It was administered by the German authorities, but the junior officers were Italian. Cassati was one of them. But his behaviour must have been condoned; he had too many victims for it all to go unnoticed.'

'Someone has certainly taken an exact revenge. Cassati must have died, like his victims, in agony of mind.'

'It is tragic. Because you, see, Superintendent, he felt no penitence. Even a week ago, when he had everything the world could offer, he could not spare the time to feel sorrow that he had deprived so many of their world.'

'I can see that you had reason to hate him.'

'I did not hate him.'

Simon was startled.

'Then why...?'

'I wished to speak to him,' she went on, not noticing the interruption, 'to assure him that after a great deal of struggling and of prayer I was able to forgive him his terrible crime if only he could, even at this late time, repent of it. But when I told him my business, he refused to give me his attention. I am hardly surprised that he did not wish to recall and discuss the subject, but, in the circumstances, I deeply regret that I did not force him to do so.'

Simon sat thoughtfully in silence. All this business about repentance and forgiveness sounded most unlikely, although of course the unlikely had an unpleasant habit of being true. The manner of Cassati's death, and especially the presence of the dagger, could only be explained by the fact that the murderer knew what Mrs Sheraton-Smith had just described. Yet she could not possibly have been the driver of the Daimler. Had she used her money to hire a murderer? If so, had she herself travelled in the car to assist her employee? Now that the significance of the dagger was known, of course, there was no longer any need to suppose two attackers; the knife could have been thrown down the dene-hole after the victim was already there. It was worth a check, however.

'How did you travel home after you left Cassati on Christmas Eve?'

'By taxi.'

'From the Opera House?'

'Yes. I walked round to the front.'

Simon made a note to check with all taxi-drivers who normally awaited the end of the opera.

'Did any of your staff see you when you arrived home?'

'No. The cook goes early to bed and Mary had gone home for Christmas. I can assure you, however, that I came straight here on that evening. I was deeply distressed.'

'Have you a car of your own?'

'No. I find it simpler to use taxis than to employ a chauffeur.'

'I see. Are there any circumstances, Mrs Sheraton-Smith, in which you consider murder to be justified?'

'None. As it happens, I strongly disapprove of the death penalty being inflicted by the State, and I certainly would not condone the taking of life by any private person.'

'Did you have any prior knowledge, even any suspicion, that this particular murder was about to take place?'

'None.'

'And you were not concerned with it in any way?'

'I can see that I must seem to you to have a reason for hatred, Superintendent, but I had nothing to do with this death.'

'This is my last question, Mrs Sheraton-Smith. Did Mr Tredegar know what you have told me?'

'Not from me,' she answered with some surprise. 'I can see no reason why he should know, or why he should be interested in the matter. I hardly think that he had any relations in the camp.'

'Thank you very much. I must apologise most sincerely for the distress I have caused you.'

'I appreciate your motives, Superintendent. Doubtless you will soon reach the end of your search.'

It seemed to Simon as he walked away an unlikely possibility. Even as he congratulated himself that the death of Owen Burr could now be treated as an accident, the thought occurred to him that, on the contrary, the murder of Cassati might be only a red herring, designed to suggest to him just that conclusion. He dismissed the thought almost before he had weighed it; the blood of the murderer could surely not be as cold as that.

A telephone booth caught his attention and he phoned through to Sergeant Flint, instructing him to start the check on the Covent Garden taxi-drivers. The sergeant had some news to give.

'Dr Smiles telephoned five minutes ago, sir, from the hospital. He said that Mr Tredegar has recovered consciousness but he's afraid that it's only a matter of minutes before he dies.'

Simon waited for nothing more. This was one time, he decided, when a taxi fare on his expense sheet would be approved. He sat impatiently on the edge of his seat until they reached the hospital; then within a moment he was outside

Evan Tredegar's room. The man whom he had posted there rose quietly to his feet.

'Dr Smiles would like a word before you go in, sir. He's in the next room.'

Simon hurried in. The doctor's face was grave.

'Good morning, Superintendent. Mr Tredegar became conscious for the first time half an hour ago. I have not attempted to discuss the accident with him. I wouldn't let you do so if there were any hope, but I'm afraid his heart is failing fast; all you can affect is the time. How long you will have depends on how much you excite him; it will be less than half an hour. He can't speak, I'm afraid, but he's recovered a little move-ment in his right hand. You'll have to do the best you can with that. I'm sorry there's nothing I can do to help.'

Simon nodded and went into the next room where Evan Tredegar lay motionless, his right hand lying heavy on top of the sheet. Simon put his own hand inside it. The old man's eyes opened painfully; he looked at his visitor, but no muscle of his face moved in recognition.

'You remember me,' said Simon. 'I'm the detective who plagued you, and now I want to find out something about this unfortunate accident of yours. If you can hear and understand what I say, will you press my hand?'

The pressure was slow but definite. Simon smiled his thanks.

'Good. Now, if you want to answer "yes" to any question, will you squeeze just like that. For "no", don't move your hand at all.'

The pressure was repeated; the old man had understood.

'Did you turn on the gas fire in your room that night?'

There was no movement. *No.*

'Did you wake up to find gas in the room?'

Yes.

'So you got out of bed to turn it off and then collapsed?'

Yes.

'Could the gas have been left on by accident?'

No movement.

'Did you shut your bedroom windows tightly before you went to bed?'

Again, *no*.

'Did you hear anyone moving in your room during the night, or any sound of someone opening and shutting the window?'

No.

Simon paused. He could go no further in this direction. He moved to another subject.

'Last night I told you Mrs Bainsbury's version of your relationship and you promised to give me the true version. Were you ever in love with her?'

There was no pressure from the heavy cold hand.

'Was she, as a young woman, in love with you?'

Yes.

'And she has continued to be anxious for your attention, without any encouragement from you?'

Yes.

'Is that all you wanted to tell me on that subject?'

There was a pause but at last the pressure came again.

'Except as a singer, did you know anything particular about Cassati?'

No.

Again Simon paused. The pressure was growing weaker and the dying man's eyelids had closed again over his tired eyes. He must come quickly to the point.

'Mr Tredegar, you must tell me this. Did you see anything during the performance of your Mass which made you suspect, even if not until later, the identity of Owen's murderer?'

The huge body, until that moment motionless, began to move with the exertion of heavy breathing. Simon recognised the violence of the feelings which could not be expressed and spoke again quickly.

'I'm not expecting you to be sure or definite—even the vaguest idea might be of help. Have you such an idea?'

There was calm again as Simon felt the movement in his hand, but it was now very faint.

'Do you think the same person might have attempted to gas you—just possibly?'

Yes.

'Mr. Tredegar, I must know who that person is. I am going to say the letters of the alphabet slowly. Will you press my hand when I come to the first letter of his name?'

As he began to recite the letters, he wished he had asked first whether it was a man or woman. But seconds were important now and he must not confuse the dying man by changing his questions. He went on slowly.

'E. F. G. H. I. J.'

His hand was gripped tightly, with more force than he had believed still to rest in that inert body.

'Does the name begin with J?' he asked, excited.

There was no relaxation of the tight grip. In sudden realisation Simon felt for the pulse in the wrist which lay so close to his own. It was not to be found. Evan Tredegar was dead.

CHAPTER TWENTY-ONE

Simon sat for a moment without moving. He had received the pressure for which he asked at the letter J, but was that now worth anything? It might have been nothing but a dying spasm from a man who could not wait until a later letter was reached. It might equally mean that an earlier letter had been passed without comment by a man who no longer had any control over even this last of his movements. Even if he, Simon, were to think that he had been given a piece of significant information, it was too easy to see what pleasure this point would give to a defending counsel. Regretfully he decided that he must forget it. Now that it was too late his mind was busy with questions which he might more profitably have asked. He rose heavily to his feet.

After a few words with Dr Smiles he walked slowly down to the entrance hall. The sound of a voice he knew asking after Evan Tredegar made him pause. He listened to the solemn answer before he took a silent step forward. Mrs Bainsbury stood there alone, her face white, her hands nervously clenching and unclenching. Suddenly she seemed to make up her mind about something; she turned abruptly and hurried out of the hospital. Simon, not knowing why he should be curious, followed.

Once outside, he faltered for a moment; missing lunch was becoming too frequent an occurrence. But Mrs Bainsbury's determined hurry drew him on. He followed her to the nearest station and found a seat from which he could watch her through the end window as she sat in the next coach of the Underground train. Her journey was to Baker Street, from which she walked steadily eastwards, Simon always discreetly behind. She turned down Harley Street, then off it, standing for a few seconds in front of a house which, in defiance of topography, bore a Harley Street number.

She summoned her courage—Simon could see her doing it—and walked up the steps. When the receptionist appeared in answer to her ring, there was a doubtful conversation before she was admitted; it seemed that she had come without an appointment. As soon as the door closed behind her Simon came closer. The profession of the house-owner could be taken as certain but there was no nameplate to give more definite information. He made a note of the number and walked briskly away in search of food.

Half an hour later, refreshed in body although still uncertain in mind, he was able to discover from a street directory that Mrs Bainsbury had been visiting a certain Dr Leo Leib. A telephone call to a friend of his who worked on one of the medical journals was even more informative.

'Leo Leib? Yes, I can tell you about him. Er—you're not enquiring on your own account, are you?'

Simon assured him that his interest was purely professional and was amused at the relief which was promptly expressed.

'Well, this chap's got quite a reputation, in a specialised sort of way. He has got various Continental medical qualifications and that's why he calls himself a doctor, but he practises chiefly as a psychiatrist. Concentrates on homosexuals; I think he works in with the police quite a lot—you know, takes over these people who are let off on condition they have treatment. With a man who's willing to be helped he can work wonders. He'll tell you anything you want to know himself, though. He came over as a refugee in the thirties and had a certain amount of official help in settling down, so he's always anxious to oblige. Like me. Okay?'

'Okay,' said Simon, and within ten minutes he was presenting himself as yet another unexpected visitor.

He was shown straight in, after he had promised the receptionist that he would leave before the next patient arrived at three o'clock. Dr Leib was a good-looking man with tired, smiling eyes and an accent attractively Austrian. Simon introduced himself as a detective.

'I imagine you usually ask most of the questions here. I hope you will answer one or two for me now.'

'I shall be happy to help you if I can, Superintendent.'

'I'm inquiring about Mrs Bainsbury, who called on you about an hour ago.'

The Austrian seemed about to deny this; then he looked quizzically at Simon.

'A woman of about fifty, in a brown coat and black hat?'

'That's right.'

'To me she gave the name Mrs Williams, but it must be the same. All my other patients today have been men.'

'I don't want to set you an ethical problem, Doctor, but if you could tell me why she needed to consult you it might be extremely valuable to me. I should explain that I am investigating three murders and I have a natural anxiety lest the third should not prove to be the last.'

'I do not think that I need have any scruples about answering your questions, as I gave a warning that I should do so if they were ever asked. It was about a question of murder that Mrs Williams came to me and I made it clear to her that I could not guarantee in advance to work against the police in a matter of that sort. She was in a state of considerable anxiety. She put to me the case of a friend of hers. This friend, it appeared, had all her life been perfectly normal, until she had suffered a very severe shock. Even after that she had shown few signs of abnormality until something happened to remind her of the shock she had undergone, when she committed a murder—only one was mentioned—to free herself from the memory. Mrs Williams knew that her friend had done this, but did not wish to inform the police as she hoped that this sudden madness was only temporary, caused by circumstances which could not possibly occur again. But just in case it should not after all be only temporary, she wanted me to cure her friend.'

'What did you tell her?'

'My answer, I fear, was not what had been hoped for. I told Mrs Williams that her friend must come to me voluntarily and must accept the possibility that I might find it necessary to insist that she should remain under supervision while I examined and treated her, perhaps for a long period of time. You will understand, Superintendent, that if the friend should prove to be a homicidal maniac, I could not allow her, as my patient, to remain in society.'

'And what was Mrs Bains—Mrs Williams's reaction to that?'

'She said it was impossible. She cried for a little and then she went out. I asked her to come and see me again, but she did not answer.'

'And you let her go?'

'I will be honest with you, Superintendent. I did not believe a word of her story. You tell me that murder has in fact been committed, so I am wrong, but she appeared to me to be a woman capable of considerable self-deception and at present— perhaps constantly—in a state of suppressed hysteria. Certainly she needs psychiatric treatment, but it is not a matter of life and death to her and my fees are high; nor am I a specialist in her particular trouble. I could not compel her to stay.'

'It is quite possible that her story is true. You say that this friend was a woman?'

'Do not be misled by that, Superintendent. More than half my patients come to me first with stories of "a friend". Always the friend's problems are their own. If there really is a friend in this case it could just as well have been a man; if she had any particular reason for choosing me rather than any other doctor it is possible that the friend is a male homosexual. The pronoun in the story is immaterial. The sick of mind know best how hurtful the truth can be. So you see, I have not helped you at all.'

Simon nodded wryly in agreement.

'Do you think that the woman you saw could have committed murder herself?'

The psychiatrist shook his head protestingly.

'It would be irresponsible of me to answer that question. I am sorry.'

It was the end of the interview. Simon thanked him and left thoughtfully. He had one more call to make before he returned to his office.

The call was at the War Office, and, when the doorkeeper asked his business, he named a friend, Tim Milligan, rather than try to find out which particular department he really wanted. He had worked with Tim, a Security Officer, during the war and remembered hopefully the invariable reply to any awkward request, 'Doubtless it can be arranged.'

Tim was drinking tea with his left hand while he sorted through a pile of photographs with his right. He welcomed his old colleague exuberantly and at once rang for more tea. It came accompanied by an enormous piece of cake.

'My typist's birthday,' Tim explained. 'She showers cake on anyone who comes in out of the sheer joy of being a year older. Makes me feel a cad every year because I never remember and by tea-time it's too late even to find a bunch of flowers some-where. However, what can I do for you?'

'I want some dope about a prisoner-of-war camp in Italy. I know it's not your department, but I thought you might be able to put me on the right track.'

'I can do better than that. I can arrange for it to become my department as from now. Everyone accepts the fact—unwillingly—that Security is liable to stick its nose into anything at any time. Which camp was it?'

Simon fished in his wallet for the details which Mrs Shera-ton-Smith had written down for him and handed them over. Tim phoned them down to Records and the two men chatted until a girl appeared, trying to keep the dust of a file away from her overall.

'Now, what do you want to know?'

'First of all, I want to confirm that a young fellow called Geoffrey Sheraton-Smith died in the camp.'

'Rank and regiment?'

'Lieutenant. Sorry, I forgot to ask about the regiment.'

'Never mind.' Tim found the place and whistled softly. 'My God, the place can't have been very healthy. There's a death roll as long as my arm.' He turned back a few pages. 'Oh, I see. There was a case put up against one of the junior camp officers as a war criminal, but they don't seem to have caught up with him.'

'What was his name?'

'Pulvi. Nasty-looking bit of work. Look.'

Simon leaned over to see. The photograph, taken from a military identity card, was faded and had never been clear, but its subject was Cassati. It was a thinner, grimmer Cassati, looking villainous in a slovenly cap, but there was no mistaking the glinting, pig-like eyes and the thick-lipped mouth.

'That's one case you can close,' said Simon. 'The man's dead; that's why I'm here. I suppose he changed his name when Italy packed in, to avoid trial. And once he'd started to make an international reputation, he'd want to keep that part of his life as dark as possible. Anyway, it's his victims I want to trace.'

'Sheraton-Smith, you said. Yes, he's here. Aged twenty.'

'She was telling the truth, then. I heard this afternoon how the boy died.' He repeated what he had learned. 'And this man, Pulvi—Cassati—was killed more or less by the same method; almost a judicial execution, in a way. Can I have a look at the complete list of the dead?'

'Of course, but it's a long one. I'll check through with you. Is there any particular name you hope to find?'

'All I can hope is that one of them will ring a bell as I read it. But I might be interested in, say, an older man called Southerley.'

They read down the sad list together, but Tim's attention wandered. He stared out of the window while Simon worked methodically on.

'Look here,' he said slowly at last. 'How did your old lady know all this about the way her boy died? It's true, all right, but how did she find out?'

Simon put his finger on the line and looked up.

'I presume the War Office told her when they had to report him dead.'

Tim banged a protesting fist down on the table.

'Use your nut, Simon. Do you really think that we'd send a mother an official report of how her son was slowly murdered? All she'd get from us would be a "Died of Wounds" or "Shot while escaping" or something like that. If a senior officer did send a letter afterwards, he'd definitely make the death sound quick and easy; if he wasn't prepared to do that, he wouldn't write at all. No censorship would allow that sort of news out of the camp at the time, either. Someone's gone out of his way to distress her since then.'

'Of course,' said Simon after a moment's thought. 'Where's a list of the men who went to the camp and survived?'

Tim found the place in the file. Simon began to read, but he had not gone very far before he looked up, his face pale and grave.

'It's time I went back on the beat,' he said. 'I could have found this out quite simply without troubling you at all. May I use your phone?'

Tim nodded, and listened with some curiosity to the one side of the conversation which followed.

'Mrs Sheraton-Smith? This is Superintendent Hudson here. I'm very sorry indeed, but I have to ask you one or two further questions relative to the death of your son. Did you know when you offered to share the payment of Cassati's fee that he was Geoffrey's murderer?'

'When did you find out, then?'

'Mrs Sheraton-Smith, who told you?'

There was a long silence on Simon's part, although Tim had heard that the answer was short.

'And this was on the day after the Mass was performed. How were you told? Calmly, or excitedly?'

'So you think that the sight of Cassati himself may have had an unbalancing effect?'

'I see. Thank you very much, Mrs. Sheraton-Smith.'

He rang off and Tim looked at him curiously.

'Well?'

Simon pointed to a name on the list in front of him.

'I've found the executioner.'

CHAPTER TWENTY-TWO

Simon knocked impatiently at Mrs Bainsbury's front door. He had knocked before, but although there had been no answer, no sound from the house, he was convinced that it was not empty. For a third time he knocked sharply and often and this time the door was opened—by one of his own men, whom he had sent round behind the house.

'The back door was unlocked, sir, and I could hear that you weren't having any luck. There's a kettle on the boil, so there should be someone around.'

Simon nodded and stepped inside. He tried first the door of Roger's little room, but it revealed nothing. Next he entered the drawing-room. He saw Mrs Bainsbury at once. She was sprawled across the sofa, her shoulders shaking as she buried her face in a cushion which subdued the noise of her sobbing. Before Simon had time to speak, she became aware of his presence and lifted her head to look at him. Her face was pale and ugly with tears, her eyes wild with despair.

'I don't know what to do,' she cried. 'I don't know what to do.'

Simon took no notice of her distress.

'There is nothing you can do,' he said. 'Where is your son?'

There was horror in her eyes as she realised what he meant; then the despair returned as she accepted what she had already known, that she had failed finally to save her son.

'He's in his bedroom,' she said quietly. 'He went up with a headache when he got back from work and I locked him in. I was afraid—I didn't know what to do.'

'Stay here, please,' Simon said sharply and hurried up the stairs, followed by the constable. He returned to the drawing room five minutes later, alone.

'They won't hang him, will they?' whispered Mrs Bainsbury. 'He's mad, you know. That terrible man has made him mad.'

'They won't hang him,' Simon said briefly. He sat down and looked at her unsmilingly. 'Now Mrs Bainsbury, I want to hear all that you know. Nothing you say is going to make any difference. Are you ready to answer my questions?'

She nodded silently.

'When did you first find out that your son had met Cassati before?'

'About a fortnight before the concert, Roger asked me whether it would be possible to stop him coming. He seemed very upset about the matter, but he didn't give me any reasons and I hardly felt I could do anything about it. He only told me the whole story on Christmas Day, and then it was too late. I could tell then, from the way he talked, that he was—well, not quite normal. When I heard about Geoffrey, though, it seemed to me that there were good reasons why Roger should have been upset; I thought perhaps he might be able to forget the whole thing now it was over, and I was sure he wasn't an ordinary murderer. It was only when he caused Evan's death, so unnecessarily, that I knew something would have to be done.'

'Why did you not go to the police on Christmas Day?'

'I have told you. Besides, you would not really expect a mother to give up her son for the sake of such a monster.'

'But if you had come forward at once, Cassati's life might have been saved. He did not die immediately. Did you know before Christmas Day that it was Roger who had killed Owen Burr?'

'I didn't know what to think. You see, he wasn't supposed to be at the concert at all; he had told me that he would be staying on to a party after his soccer match at Oxford. That was why he came to the rehearsal in the morning. But at the rehearsal, of course, he saw Cassati, and the whole thing seemed to boil over in his mind. He told me that he couldn't bear to think that so pure a sound could come from so foul a man; it seemed to him important that he should stop it. He was playing in a match at Oxford that afternoon, but he broke away from the party early. He had a gun here which he brought home after the war, and just the single bullet it was loaded with. He collected that and then went on to the Festival Hall, arriving about ten minutes before the end of the performance; he stood in the doorway where Evan Tredegar was already listening. I saw him there— Roger, I mean; I was telling the truth when I said that I didn't see Evan. They must have changed places in the minute before Delia looked.'

'Mr Tredegar knew that Roger was there, then?'

'Yes. Roger muttered something about coming to meet me, I gather, and hoped that it would be taken as quite natural. Evan left just before the end, so he didn't see Roger fire. But of course if he had mentioned the meeting to you, it would have been awkward; and that evening when you came here Roger thought he was inviting you round so that he could tell you about it. That was why…'

She began to cry again, but Simon gave her no time.

'So you guessed at once, did you, that Roger had shot Owen? Was that why you wrote the letter to me?'

'I didn't know till Christmas. I didn't know the facts about Cassati, and I couldn't think why Roger should want Owen to die. But I thought it was strange, Roger turning up like that, and, when I asked him, he said he hadn't been there. So I was afraid he might possibly have had something to do with it. I was worried about it, especially when I heard that you suspected Evan.'

'Did Roger feel any regret when he realised that he had killed Owen by mistake?'

'I don't think he did,' she replied hesitantly. 'That evening was the first time when, even without knowing what had happened, I wondered whether he was quite normal. He said then that the music had excited him, but afterwards he told me that he was just furiously angry with Owen for having suddenly moved into such an unlikely position. That first failure upset him so much that the next day he did one completely stupid thing. He told Janet—Janet Sheraton-Smith—the truth about Cassati and Geoffrey; I suppose you know that, but I only found out from her this morning and I was terribly frightened that Roger might try to harm Janet as well as Evan. But perhaps he was so unbalanced at the time that afterwards he forgot he had spoken to her. Today he seemed to be behaving queerly again, though; I suppose he was wondering whether Evan had said anything.'

'Have you ever noticed any signs of abnormality in your son before, Mrs Bainsbury?'

Again she hesitated.

'Well, there was something. I suppose it was my fault, and of course his father died while he was still a boy. But I did know that his friendship with Geoffrey Sheraton-Smith was very close; their housemaster told me about it. I thought they'd grow out of it, though, they were only boys. But as soon as they left school, they were thrown into the Army, and, before they had time to settle down in it, they were prisoners—and still so young, Superintendent. They were together all the time, so it's hardly surprising—and then Roger had to watch his friend being killed like that! It must have been a terrible experience. When he came back, he tried very hard to be— well, an ordinary young man. He used to take girls out, and I always hoped that one of them might be able to help him; but I don't think he would ever let them. But why do you want all this second-hand information? Why don't you ask Roger himself?'

'I am not able to do so, Mrs Bainsbury.' He stared at her for a moment, wondering how much had happened with her knowledge; but the puzzled expression of her eyes convinced him, and he spoke more compassionately. 'Did you not know when you locked him in that your son kept his spare razor blades in his bedroom?'

She understood him at once and stood up, white-faced.

'Is he dead?'

'I'm afraid so, Mrs Bainsbury. But perhaps it is the best solution. You mustn't be too upset.'

There was a very long pause before she spoke quietly.

'Is a mother to smile when her son dies? I would like you to go now, Superintendent.'

He nodded sympathetically.

'I will leave you. One of my men will have to stay until the ambulance comes, but I will tell him not to disturb you. You too must have had a terrible experience in these last few days.'

He left her to face the tragedy of her future life and, suddenly depressed, went to Delia for comfort.

* * *

DELIA LISTENED in silence as Simon talked; occasionally, her face troubled, she leaned forward to stab an unnecessary poker into the fire.

'Poor Roger,' she said when he had finished. 'And poor Mrs Bainsbury. It must have been terrible for her. Was Roger really the only one concerned? I mean, did he manage to kill Cassati single-handed?'

'Well, he didn't actually strike a killing blow, but he did everything else. He was fit, and, though Cassati was a heavy man, he was flabby, and he was a coward. Roger had fixed the doors and windows of the Daimler and the glass partition behind the driver to turn the back of the car into a little gas chamber. That gave him the opportunity to tie his victim up. And afterwards, you have to remember that Cassati didn't know anything about the dene-holes. When he found himself being marched into the darkness of the wood, he may have believed that there would still be time to turn and fight.'

'It's horrible, isn't it?' Delia shivered as her imagination brought the scene to life. 'But at least it's all finished now. Are all your questions answered? What about the two washed-up glasses, for instance?'

'We shan't ever know for certain,' Simon said. 'Roger may not have had anything to do with them, though. I was speaking to Dr Smiles this morning and he suggested one possible explanation. Apparently, the Old Man had been forbidden to drink port, so perhaps he washed the glasses up himself, lest Annie should tell the doctor. It sounds silly, but old men do sometimes behave like that.'

'And the gun?' Delia asked. 'I suppose Roger slipped that into John's coat while we were all at the committee meeting.'

'He must have done. It looks as though John was telling nothing but the truth all along.'

Delia refrained from saying, 'I told you so'. She was still looking unhappy.

'You know I was fond of Roger once, don't you?'

'Yes, I know,' he said quietly.

'And yet I never guessed that he could do a thing like this.'

'Why should you guess? Even his mother didn't know until he told her. None of us knew just from looking at him.'

'But I knew him better than that. He used to talk about himself a lot; I knew some of his difficulties, but I never suspected that he could behave, or even think, in such a way.'

Simon moved to sit on the arm of her chair.

'I don't quite understand what's worrying you, Delia. No one blames you for not recognizing a potential murderer.'

'It's not for that I blame myself. It's something else. Simon, you were quite right when you told me that no one could be sure, even of the person he loved. I didn't believe you, but you were right, and I was wrong. I'm sorry I was angry. Will you forgive me, Simon?'

It was the question that he had waited himself to ask and to hear answered for so many days. 'With all my heart,' he said. 'And now, with all my heart, there's a question that I want to ask you.'

ANSWER
IN THE
NEGATIVE

CHAPTER ONE

'More coffee, darling?' asked Sally Heldar.

'Yes, please. It seems particularly good tonight.'

'Because we don't always have it,' said Sally, thinking of the price. She refilled Johnny's cup, returned it to him, and sat comfortably back in her chair.

The house was quiet after a busy day. It was a little Regency house in St Cross Square — a peaceful Bloomsbury backwater which had somehow escaped transformation into offices and private hotels. The flat which Johnny had found after the war had been very adequate until they had tried to get Peter into it too. After that they had moved, and the house held the twins and Nanny quite comfortably as well. It was, conveniently, a quarter of an hour's walk from Heldar Brothers' shop in the Charing Cross Road.

The fire was burning well. They had turned out the wall lights and were sitting under the softer glow of the standard lamps. The light fell kindly on the little Adam mantelpiece, the flowered chintzes and the Persian rug, the old rosewood and mahogany pieces which they had inherited from Mark Mercator, who had died by violence four years before. The room was extraordinarily peaceful, and when the front-door bell rang Johnny said wearily, 'Oh, damn!'

But it was no use pretending they weren't in. Anyone who knew them at all knew that there was always someone here in the evening, because of the children. Johnny got up and went out of the room.

A minute or two later Sally heard voices on the stairs. She listened, recognised the second voice, and relaxed just before Johnny opened the door again.

'It's all right,' he said. 'It's only Toby.'

'I hope you mean that kindly.' Toby Lorn looked small and slight beside Johnny. But he was well up to the middle height and by no means puny, though he was always too thin. His hair was dark and smooth, and his cheeks a little hollowed below his horn-rimmed spectacles. He looked tired, as usual. But he smiled and limped forward and kissed Sally affectionately.

'We're delighted to see you, Toby,' she said. 'Have you eaten? There's plenty in the kitchen.'

'Yes, I've eaten, thanks, Sally.'

'Would you like coffee, then — there's lots left — or will you give Johnny an excuse for a drink?'

Johnny looked at Toby's tired face. 'Have mercy on me,' he said. 'I'll get the whisky. Sit down, won't you?'

Toby thanked him and sat down on the sofa, straightening his left leg unobtrusively in its calliper. Toby was the young stepbrother of Peter Lorn, who had been at Porterbury and Magdalen with Johnny and had been killed at one of the Rhine crossings. Young Peter had been called after him. Johnny had found Toby after the war, an unhappy, sensitive sixteen-year-old, recovering slowly and without much enthusiasm from polio, debarred from most public school activities, his father recently dead and his mother clearly not much use to him. Johnny had pulled him through with infinite patience, exercised a certain amount of remote control while he was at Oxford, and seen him into Fleet Street. He was twenty-nine now, still over-sensitive under a professional armour of cynicism — few people guessed that he was the son of a country parson — but standing strongly enough on his own feet and doing pretty well.

Johnny came back with a tray and helped Toby and himself from the decanter and the syphon. They said, 'Cheers,' drank, and settled down again, and for a quarter of an hour or so the room was very quiet. Toby had plenty of conversation when it was needed — with strangers he was apt, like some other news-papermen, to be a slightly feverish conversationalist — but with the Heldars he could relax. Sally, watching him unobtrusively, saw the lines on his forehead smooth themselves out a little. She wondered again if his evening meal had consisted of sandwiches and remembered the bleakness of his flat.

Presently he put his tumbler down and turned to Johnny.

'I'm afraid I really came,' he said, 'because I wanted to consult you.'

Johnny raised an eyebrow. 'Rare book? Manuscript?'

'No. I don't want to consult you as an antiquarian book-seller; I was thinking of your other capacity.'

'Oh,' said Johnny cautiously. 'Don't tell me you've had a murder in Fleet Street.'

'Nothing so interesting, I'm afraid. It's merely a poison-pen in the office.'

Johnny's nostrils twitched a little. 'Not very nice,' he said. 'I'm sorry for you. But poison-pens are rather outside my expe-rience, Toby.'

'I know — at least, I was afraid you'd say so. But will you listen to the story?'

'Certainly.'

'Thank you.' Toby paused to collect his thoughts, and then began.

'I think I'd better explain the set-up first. As you may or may not remember, we're called the National Press Archives. We're a fairly new concern — we only opened six months ago. The Loughbridge Commission on the Press was largely responsible for our foundation, and the Treasury put up part of the money. The object of the exercise was to provide easy access to newspaper cuttings and pictures — photographs and old prints and engravings and so on — for Fleet Street and authors and business firms, and indeed almost anyone. The Fleet Street agencies deposit their stuff with us as soon as its immediate news value has worn off. We make no charge for letting people see a picture or a cutting, but we take a minimum of thirty shillings for any picture which is reproduced. We don't own any copyrights — the agencies didn't want to give them up — so a percentage of the charge goes to the owners. The Archives are divided into two departments, known locally as Feelthee Peex and Comic Cuts, with a Negative Department as a subsidiary to Peex.

'We're housed in the new *Echo* building in Fleet Street. It's a little large for the *Echo*, so they let some of it to us. Peex and Cuts are on the sixth floor, which is the top, and we have basement-room for negatives and messenger boys. You don't want to keep negs in the same place as pix; it's putting all your eggs in one basket, because there's always a risk of fire.'

'I'm putting all my negs in one basket,' murmured Johnny outrageously, with a hint of the Fred Astaire tune.

'Darling, *really*!' said Sally, and Toby groaned.

'Sorry,' said Johnny. 'Couldn't resist it. Go on.'

Toby went on. 'All our printing, and photo-statting of cuttings, is done by the *Echo*'s dark-room — on a business footing, of course. Also, we are allowed to use the *Echo*'s very excellent canteen.' He paused and lit a cigarette.

'So far, the Archives have proved a reasonably successful experiment. But we're not an altogether happy office, principally because we're a mixture of Fleet Street and Civil Service. The Archivist — the man who runs the whole thing — is a Civil Servant. His name is Lionel Silcutt, and the story goes that he was swaddled in red tape at birth. He means extremely well, and he's really rather a nice man. But he can't get on with the present head of Comic Cuts, who is a pure-blooded newspaperman and Irish at that — a man called Michael Knox.'

'The man who wrote for the *Sunday Reflector?*' asked Johnny.

'The same. To my mind he made the *Reflector* — he's a brilliant writer and a brilliant controversialist — and the circulation has dropped since he left. He's an infuriating creature, but Fleet Street will put up with almost any eccentricities in a man who can really write, and I don't think they'd ever have sacked him. He had a stupendous row with his editor about six weeks ago, knocked him down, and walked out. At that time his predecessor in the Archives, who was another dyed-in-the-wool Fleet Street type, had just handed in his resignation because he couldn't get on with Silcutt. Michael thought he'd like the job because he's writing a book and he wanted regular pay and hours which would leave him time for it — and easy access to pix for it. I'm not quite sure why Silcutt thought he would like Michael, but Michael was recommended by James Camberley. It was generous of Camberley, because Mike had just been slating him a bit in the *Reflector*. He's very seldom wrong about a man, and I'm inclined to think still that Mike may have got something — something for us, I mean. He's still on his month probation — everyone has to do that — and I wouldn't be surprised if Silcutt gave him a bit longer. To return to the general set-up — I seem to be wandering a bit — he has eight assistants and three typists under him.

'The head of Feelthee Peex is me. I can take it — more or less — because I'm something of a hybrid. I came to Fleet Street partly because I was still reacting against a clerical background, and I still like the free-and-easiness of it. But a year or so ago I began to react the other way and hanker after discipline and regular hours. So I took this job when it came along, and on the whole I like it. I temper it with the odd bit of newspaper work. I

have a staff of eleven assistants and three typists. I am also —
rather embarrassingly — set over the Negatives Department.
The staff there consists of Miss Quimper and four assistants —
no typists; they have very little typing and our girls do it for
them. Miss Quimper is a problem. To begin with she's well over
fifty and I have no right to be set over her. She also reminds me
vividly of a very devout and strong-minded church-worker of
my childhood who wanted to hear dear Tobias's catechism
every time she came to tea. But the real trouble is that she was
in the old Evans's Picture Library for over thirty years, and
although she's extremely sound in her way she's got immovably
set in it. Her methods are very horse-and-buggy and really quite
impracticable, but she won't modify them, and when thwarted
she bursts into tears.'

'My poor Toby,' said Sally. 'How very upsetting for you!'

'There is nothing more embarrassing,' said Toby, 'than
making a woman cry. It makes one feel like a monster. To
continue, however.'

But he didn't continue at once. He hesitated for a moment or
two. Then he said a little abruptly, 'There's one other person of
importance. A man in Peex called Frank Morningside. He's
neither fish nor fowl — neither Civil Service nor Fleet Street —
but several other people on the staff are in the same position
and don't find it a handicap. He went to a grammar school and a
provincial University. A lot of other people went to a grammar
school and no University at all, and neither they nor we find it a
cause of embarrassment. But Morningside has all sorts of pecu-
liar ideas about public-school types. He was just too young for
the war, and did his National Service without distinction, as far
as anyone knows. Then, when he'd taken his degree, he taught
for several years, and came to this job from that, because he
wanted a change. Or possibly because his last job was at a prep
school, and he couldn't cope with the brats.'

Toby broke off again. The lines were back in his forehead,

and he was concentrating hard — making a sharp effort of some sort. When he spoke again every trace of cynicism had gone from his voice.

'There's nothing wrong with him. He has no vices — I'm quite sure of that. He doesn't drink — except beer; he doesn't smoke, and his life is wide open to anyone who cares to look. He's intoler— he's very smug. He has no sense of humour, but that isn't his fault. He's very good indeed at his job — very steady and methodical. He also has a superb visual memory, which is a great asset in a place like ours. We've taken over a lot of old pix and negs from Evans's and one or two other picture libraries — mostly unidentified stuff salvaged during the Blitz — and he's very clever at spotting well-known people and places in them. He wants to syndicate a sort of "Myself when Young" series — Churchill in a sailor-suit, and Lloyd George in golden ringlets, and so on. The typists call him the Memory Man. There is no doubt that he's an admirable person. There is no doubt that he's a very irritating one, too. But that's no reason for writing him filthy letters.'

There was a short silence. Then Toby went on again, his voice tired now, as if his effort had been a little too much for him.

'It started in a perfectly harmless way, about a month ago. Someone left a rude rhyme on his desk. It was typed on a torn-off piece of office paper. It was quite funny, but not all that clever, and not all that rude either. I can't remember it now. Morningside didn't see the joke. Then he received another, slightly more ribald, but still quite mild, and he was definitely annoyed. And then other things began to happen — silly, irritating things. Someone patronised a joke shop — there's one quite near us, incidentally, in St Barnabas' Lane. Morningside would find blobs of ink on the pix he was going to send out, and they'd turn out to be tin. He opened his desk drawer one day, and one of those snakes on a spring shot out. He plays squash one evening a week and brings a suitcase to the office with a pair of shorts and a sports shirt. One evening when he changed at the courts, he found itching powder in the shorts. And there were other things of the same kind. All very prep school. Meantime the rude rhymes continued and got ruder.

'I should have explained that Morningside has a small private office off Peex. So have I, and so have our typists, and we've always locked our doors at night. Our stuff isn't intrinsically valuable, but it would be tiresome and sometimes impossible to replace. The cleaners come in the morning, and they get duplicate keys from the *Echo* porters' room downstairs. But until this business started not even Morningside, who is extremely conscientious, thought of locking his door when he went to lunch, or when he left his office for a few minutes during the day. But when the persecution got really tiresome, he began to do that. It was hideously inconvenient for everyone else, because clients came in for pix which were in his office, and his telephone rang and no one could answer it, and we wanted his reference books, and so on. But it didn't last long, because it wasn't worthwhile. When his office was locked by day nothing happened. But the things began to happen by night. There was no sign of interference with the lock, so we assumed that the joker had acquired a key. The porters were questioned at once and said that to the best of their knowledge no one but the cleaners had ever had the duplicate. But it seemed quite possible that someone else — almost anyone else — had had it long enough to take an impression, or even to have a new key professionally cut. The porters' room isn't continuously occupied. Since they were questioned one of them has always carried it on him, except when the cleaners have it, but that isn't much good now.

'These investigations were made because Morningside complained to Silcutt. He might have come to me, but he thought I might be responsible for his troubles. Silcutt decided, reluctantly, that he'd better take action. He discussed it with me, and I agreed. We were both inclined to think that either the younger typists in Peex or, more likely, the messenger boys were responsible for the kid-stuff. Silcutt saw the head typist — a nice woman called Mrs Beates — and the two girls, Pat and Pam, who are a little apt to be at the bottom of any trouble. As soon as they understood it was serious, Pat and Pam admitted the two original rhymes. But they persistently denied all knowledge of the rest of it, and Silcutt was satisfied that they were telling the truth. I thought so too. He then saw the boys. There are four of them. Two are probably innocent. The third was christened — or at least registered — Gordon Parston but is known as Teddy because he is a Teddy Boy. He's a crazy mixed-up kid and a hot suspect, and the fourth boy is a buddy of his and easily led. Neither of them would admit anything, but there was a strong presumption of guilt.

'But it wasn't as simple as that. The boys might well be playing about with itching powder. But they were certainly not responsible for the written stuff. It had improved in literary quality, if in nothing else, and was undoubtedly the work of an educated person. Morningside realised that, and thought it was probably Michael Knox's or mine. Or else' — he hesitated a moment, and then went on in a carefully flat voice — 'Selina Marvell's. She's my principal assistant in Peex, and what Morningside would classify as a public-school type. She was also engaged to him recently, and he turned her down — I wouldn't know why. But he thought she might be writing the stuff out of spite.'

So that was it, thought Sally. Toby was in love with this girl with the charming name. That was why he had made his painful effort to be fair to Morningside; he hadn't wanted his portrait to be distorted or obscured by jealousy. He was carrying his passion for integrity in writing over to this story — and probably to his own emotions.

'Here's a sample,' he said, and produced a battered wallet, from which he took a piece of paper. 'One of the earlier ones. Morningside's burnt all the others. He said they were indecent.'

Johnny looked at it. 'No one thought of fingerprints, I suppose. Why should they, after all, at that stage?' He took the paper and read. He grinned once, uncontrollably, and then studied the thing carefully. After a moment he asked, 'Whom did you suspect yourself, Toby?'

'I wasn't sure. I'm still not sure. I don't think Pat and Pam have the intelligence or the literary skill. Selina certainly has.' Toby's voice was still flat. 'It seems a little too hot for her, but one never quite knows. But I thought — and I'm still inclined to think — it was probably Michael. He's quite clever enough, and the ruder stuff didn't start till after he came. And he and Morningside don't get on at all.'

'I see. Let me just get another point clear. Which actually started first, the prep school stuff or the ruder rhymes?'

Toby considered. 'The prep school stuff,' he said definitely. 'I remember because I happened to be with Morningside when the snake popped up, and that was the first incident in this second stage of the campaign. And I think an ink blob appeared before the first of the ruder rhymes, too.'

'Right. Please go on.'

'Well, then the nature of the thing changed again, but gradually this time. The prep school stuff became more serious. Real ink was spilt on Morningside's pix. Then some of them were torn up. Some of the old glass negs he was working on in his leisure moments were smashed. Then his overcoat was slashed. During the same period the ruder rhymes became ruder still, began to give evidence of an ugly mind, and finally degenerated into obscene letters. Here you are. No one thought of fingerprints on them either, I'm afraid.'

Johnny took the dirty envelope, drew out a paper, unfolded it, and read it through. He didn't smile this time.

'Quite so,' he said. 'Rather different from the earlier stuff. Cheap paper — rather cheaper than the other — and cheap envelope, both obtainable at almost any stationer's. Message and name on envelope printed in ballpoint ink, as the rhyme was, but the printing of the rhyme was educated, and this definitely isn't. Still, that doesn't mean it was done by an uneducated person. One must deduce, I suppose, that it's the effort of a well-educated degenerate.' He paused. 'All these things were left in Morningside's office, I gather, and none of them came by post? Yes.' He restored the paper to its envelope and returned it, with the ruder rhyme, to Toby. 'But, you know, the police could tell you far more about it than I can. Why not the police, Toby? It wouldn't necessarily mean publicity.'

'We're in Fleet Street,' said Toby. 'Everything gets around, and we're not much liked, because we're more or less a government concern. I had quite enough trouble persuading Silcutt and Morningside to let me talk to you. Morningside agreed because he doesn't think its respectable to be involved with the police — and because the letters are driving him nearly out of his mind. Silcutt agreed — finally — because of your amateur status. You could be consulted unofficially — a word which covers a multitude of sins. Even so he had to consult someone else about consulting you. He felt he must take it to a higher level. So I suggested he should talk to Camberley, who of course was on the Loughbridge Commission. As the *Echo*'s Lobby Correspondent, he's in and out of the building a good deal, and he takes an interest in the Archives. He said we must certainly go ahead. I gather he's met you. He gave you a very good Press.'

'That was nice of him,' said Johnny. 'He doesn't really know me — he's an occasional customer of ours. He's interested in anything we can find on North Africa.'

Toby nodded. 'That's his speciality, of course. Well, Johnny, what about it? Do you think you could help us? We should be quite enormously obliged to you.'

Johnny didn't answer at once. He sat frowning at the fire, and Toby waited patiently. He had a curious look of docile resignation — the resignation of a sick person, thought Sally. But his eyes behind his spectacles were anxious.

Johnny turned abruptly. Sally saw his face change a little. Then he said, 'All right. That is, if I'm allowed to ask questions within the Archives.'

'Oh, yes. Silcutt expects that.'

'Good. But I take it you haven't mentioned me to anyone there except Silcutt and Morningside? Then I'd like to sit about for a day or two before anyone else knows what I'm after. Perhaps I could be doing a book on something you've got plenty of stuff on.'

When Toby was really pleased his smile was surprisingly warm and wholehearted.

'That's grand,' he said. 'I'm frightfully grateful, Johnny. The entire collection of Feelthee Peex is at your disposal. We've got a lot of French stuff—' He broke off as Johnny began to laugh. 'All right, all right. I only wanted to suggest something on your own subject.'

'You're only making it worse, Toby dear,' said Sally kindly, and Toby laughed too.

He left them at half past ten, looking a little younger.

Johnny went downstairs with him. When he came back to the drawing room, he looked at Sally and said, 'Do you mind my taking on a job like this?'

'No, I don't,' she said. 'I think poison-pens are things that particularly need to be dealt with. But you weren't going to, were you?'

'No. I thought they ought to go to the police, and it did seem fairly messy. And then' — Johnny sounded slightly exasperated — 'I looked at Toby, and he looked exactly as he did when I first saw him after the war — when he was still a kid and still a bit of an invalid — and I said yes more or less without thinking. I hope it wasn't a mistake.'

'I shouldn't think so. Johnny — I've been wondering if I couldn't help you with this. If I'd be any use, that is. You can't leave the shop all day, can you?'

'No,' said Johnny, but he looked rather doubtful.

'If you mean you don't think it would be quite nice for me, that's really nonsense, darling. I don't mind.'

'Very well. Thank you, Sally. I'll tell Toby tomorrow that you're sitting in on it. I do feel that we should take the simple and obvious course of noting and recording the people who go into Morningside's office when he's not there. We may get something that way.'

Sally nodded. 'Toby's in love with this girl,' she said irrelevantly.

'The one with the attractive name? Yes, I think so. I hope to God she's not our joker.'

'Is it likely?'

'Probably not. I didn't ask him what she's like, because it would only have embarrassed him, and his opinion is obviously valueless, anyway. We shall just have to wait and see.'

WANT TO DISCOVER MORE UNCROWNED QUEENS OF CRIME?

SIGN UP TO OUR CRIME CLASSICS NEWSLETTER TO DISCOVER NEW GOLDEN AGE CRIME, RECEIVE EXCLUSIVE CONTENT, AND NEVER-BEFORE PUBLISHED SHORT STORIES, ALL FOR FREE.

FROM THE BELOVED GREATS OF THE GOLDEN AGE TO THE FORGOTTEN GEMS, BEST-KEPT-SECRETS, AND BRAND NEW DISCOVERIES, WE'RE DEVOTED TO CLASSIC CRIME.

IF YOU SIGN UP TODAY, YOU'LL GET:

1. A FREE NOVEL FROM OUR CLASSIC CRIME COLLECTION;

2. EXCLUSIVE INSIGHTS INTO CLASSIC NOVELS AND THEIR AUTHORS; AND,

3. THE CHANCE TO GET COPIES IN ADVANCE OF PUBLICATION.

INTERESTED?

IT TAKES LESS THAN A MINUTE TO SIGN UP, JUST HEAD TO

WWW.CRIMECLASSICS.CO.UK

AND YOUR EBOOK WILL BE SENT TO YOU.

facebook.com/crimeclassics
twitter.com/crimeclassics